The Dead Walk

BREAKING FATE PUBLISHING

Published by
Breaking Fate Publishing
151 N. 4th St.
Unit C
Dekalb, IL 60115

Please visit us online at http://breakingfatepublishing.com

Cover Art & Design by Willy Adkins
Cover Model: Jolie Tune
http://deviantdesiresphoto.com
Copyright © 2014

Contents

The Price of My Services by Dylan Otto Krider 3

Zero Hour by Derek Muk 25

Prisoners of Forever by Katie Jones...43

I Walk, Therefore I Am by Ryan Neil Falcone.........................59

And the Weeds Shook with Laughter by John M. Edwards 69

The Meat Lover's Special by Miracle Austin 73

The Zombie Appeal by D. E. Cowen..83

Black Friday by Willy Adkins 123

Short-term recollections of a life... by Sergio Palumbo..........141

Survival by Jason R. Davis...163

The Price of My Services
by Dylan Otto Krider

When I first got the call from Mr. Hornfeller of Hornfeller Petrochemical Company requesting my services, I was hesitant. The people I typically represent are Billionaires with a capital 'B.' As it turned out, I had just finished wrapping up a particularly successful PR campaign repositioning pig lard as "the more flavorful alternative" to canola oil, and was always open to a consultation. I will occasionally reduce my fee if the potential client has gotten themselves in a high profile enough pickle to make it worth my while, just for the extra TV time. (I have heard people say, on more than one occasion, that it was me who deserved the Oscar for orchestrating O.J. Simpson's comeback.)

I arrived at Mr. Hornfeller's beachside mansion in St. Kitts by helicopter five minutes early, and was greeted Mr. Hornfeller chomping on an unlit cigar, flanked by three suits.

"Ms. Constantine," he said, shaking my hand and introduced everyone: the stylish looking, dark skinned man to my left was hi lawyer, Mr. Papa. To my right was muscular Malay by the name of Mr. Hua from marketing, and a bespectacled Mr. Devine from research and development.

"What seems to be the problem?" I asked.

"It's more of an… obstacle," Mr. Papa said.

A servant asked us if we would like anything to drink on our way to the foyer. I caught Mr. Hornfeller making a quick glance at my legs as I sat across from him on the sofa. If this was an underage sex scandal, I'd have to stop negotiations right then. I draw the line at perverts.

"I don't know how much you know about our business, but we deal primarily with petrochemicals. As of late, we have made a name for ourselves with our innovative fuel additives. One in particular…"

I held up my hand signaling Mr. Hornfeller to stop. "I do damage control. If it's promotion you're looking for, I can make a recommendation." Promotion, particularly of a groundbreaking product, presented no challenge. I considered it beneath me, not to mention a waste of money for the client.

Mr. Hornfeller clicked the roof of his mouth with his tongue before continuing. "One in particular," he began again, "has proved particularly promising, but there's still the matter of the obstacle."

"Obstacle?" I asked.

The four men tossed glances between them like a game of hot potato. Finally, Mr. Hornfeller spoke: "We just got a fresh shipment in. Perhaps it would be easiest if we simply showed you?"

We all stood and they led me to where a trunk rested on the helipad. It was black, with stainless steel trimmings, like the kind of thing you'd expect to be housing a bomb. "Wait," I said as Mr. Hua was about to lift lid. "I should let you know that if what I'm about to see is in any way illegal, I'm under no obligation to commit perjury. I may even be obligated to report it. I'll require a

4

million dollar retainer for a no comment. If, on the other hand, you want me to report the truth in the most favorable light possible, my usual fees will apply."

"Agreed," Mr. Hornfeller said, signaling Mr. Hua to continue. He lifted the lid to reveal what it took me a moment to realize were two deteriorated human bodies crammed head-to-toe in the fetal position like a Yin Yang symbol. Their skin was wrinkled, soot black and smelled of decay. To my horror, I noticed they were quivering. One of them – the boy – turned his head and squinted his one good eye in the light, and moaned, "Help me... help me..."

I quietly shut the lid, and could feel the four men attempting to decode my expression. No one exchanged a word as sauntered back to the mansion. In the foyer, the servant was waiting for me with my drink on a silver platter; I took my Scotch and soda and claimed my seat at the couch. I set the olive on the coffee table, took a quick sip and crossed my legs – this time, Hornfeller kept his gaze on my face. "Talk to me, gentleman."

Mr. Papa swirled his drink a few times. "Do you remember reading a news story a few months back about a toxic leak in Africa?"

"That was you?"

"Uh, yes," Mr. Papa admitted.

"You may recall it suggested certain side effects...," Mr. Hua said.

That prompted Mr. Papa to break in: "All pure speculation."

Hua continued: "One of which may have included reanimating the dead."

"That's yet to be shown," Papa interjected.

"Who represented you on that one?" I asked.

"A small firm out of Texas," Mr. Hua said. "Cromwell, Harris and Associates."

I smirked. It explained how they let the situation spin out of control into wild speculation. "You get your money's worth."

"We see that now," Mr. Hornfeller said.

"As you can imagine, the company was under extreme pressure to rectify the situation," Mr. Devine said.

Papa added, "Despite the lack of any solid scientific evidence linking our product to these…"

"…resuscitations," Hua offered, gaping at me for approval. I only shrugged. It was alright.

Mr. Devine loosened his tie. "We certainly couldn't have these corpses wandering about…"
Papa raised a finger. "No one's been able to offer any proof of these so-called…"

"…reborn?" Hua offered; I winced. "Second lifers?" Better.

"So, we tried to get a handle on the situation," Devine said.

"How many of these things are still wandering around the countryside?" I asked.

"Hard to say," said Mr. Hornfeller. "We rounded up as many as we can, but a few are sure to slip through."

"That's conjecture," Mr. Papa interjected.

"And so far, this…"

"…new lease on life," Mr. Hua said, trying out the sound of it.

I nodded. It wasn't bad. "Has been limited to Mitali," I said, completing the thought.

All eyes turned to Papa, who nodded.

That was something at least. If you were going to have a human atrocity, Africa was the only way to get it fly under the radar. "So, to sum, you've got some zombies wandering around that could be linked back to your company which you've been rounding up for – what? Experiments?"

6

Mr. Devine bowed his head, looking a bit ashamed.

"Is this a problem?" Mr. Hornfeller asked.

"Nothing insurmountable." I ran my finger along my bottom lip until I realized I was starting to arouse Mr. Devine. We'd have to figure out some way to deal with them. "We have to assume the story will break eventually, and will want to reframe the issue into a net positive by the time it does."

Mr. Hornfeller leaned back and slapped his knees and grinned. "Does this mean you'll take the job?"

"It certainly presents a fascinating challenge," I said.

* * * *

People wonder how I can represent the people I do. I could tell you I'm an advocate in the court of public opinion and everyone deserves a fair trial. You might believe that, or assume it's just another piece of spin. I might even believe it myself, and it still might not be anything more than an elaborate rationalization for my greed. I could tell you honesty is an illusion, and cite scientific studies to back me up when I tell you our brains were not made for ascertaining the world as it is, but selling ourselves.

Whether or not you believe that study will mostly depend on whether or not it conflicts with your beliefs. If, for example, you cling to the Enlightenment ideal, I could produce another study that tells you we are rational creatures, we value truth, that fact matters more to us than fiction, and that's the one you'd choose to believe. If spin is your trade, then believing once we became social animals, those better able to sway people had an advantage will appeal to you.

Whether or not you can accept what I just said is immaterial. Any answer I give to you is equally meaningless. If you want to determine if what I'm saying is true, the only thing you need to know is that I was able to build a personal portfolio bigger than many of the companies I represent. Then ask yourself, what understanding of human nature do I possess that makes that possible?

And there's your answer.

* * * *

Any company that wants to play in the big leagues has to first have its own grassroots organization, so I naturally called Fio, my go-to guy for all my populist AstroTurf. He was particularly adept at maintaining blogs to shill our in-house science studies that contradicted whatever the EPA was saying about our clients.

It was a delicate balancing act, getting ourselves an assured enough footing to break the story without taking so long to prepare that we allowed word to get out on its own.

Fortunately, the outbreak appeared to be confined to the one off-shore operation in Mitali, an African nation that, as luck would have it, had recently undergone a rather nasty ethnic cleansing. That meant a corrupt and weakened government coupled with an unstable environment for outside media.

"Turns out there's a lot of Muslims in Africa," Fio said. "Who knew?"

I had only met Fio in person once. He looked about like what you'd expect to be living in the basement of his parent's home. To look at him, you would have no idea he was one of the highest paid PR people in the business, which is exactly what you wanted in your bankrolled underwear warriors.

"You're thinking of going with the terrorism angle?" A little cliché, but I was willing to hear him out.

"I was thinking I stumble on some evidence Al Qaeda is working on a way to bring back the dead so they could engage in suicide missions *ad infinitum*," Fio said.

I was somewhat concerned about the possible cognitive dissonance of bombers leaving enough of a corpse behind for a second go, but Fio had a sixth sense about how far he could push these things. I don't like to discuss specific projects, but let's just say trusted his judgment implicitly ever since he managed to tar a particular politician as being at once an atheist, Muslim and closet Scientologist in the sway of radical Christian fundamentalists – and have his readership asserting all three simultaneously.

"Make it Iran. Otherwise, I'll defer to your judgment on this one," I said. A terrorist threat breaks out in Mitali, and who just happens to be there with their own private security force protecting their refineries? It could work.

Once the dead were a threat and had been adequately de-humanized, we could pretty much do anything we wanted with them. The question was, what?

I dialed Devine. "Do the Munches eat?" I asked. I called them that because their sunken faces reminded me of Edvard Munch's painting *The Scream*.

"No," Devine answered. "The blood's been drained, so even if they could digest anything there's no way to transport nutrients. Some of their stomachs have been opened and it – *whoosh* – passes right through."

"So what's powering them?"

"That's the thing. We've had Munches running treadmills for weeks, and they continue to decay, but they don't starve."

A pathway out of the wilderness was starting to present itself. "What you're saying is these things never have to refuel?"

"Essentially. Which would seem to violate the conservation of energy and… I don't know how much you know about physics, Ms. Constantine, but that just shouldn't be. It's very disturbing."

"You should look into that further."

"Oh, believe me, I am."

* * * *

We had already shifted operations to Hornfeller's Pishon oil refinery in Mitali. So far, the situation had been confined to some pocket sightings of zombies easily attributed to Turiya rebels.

Hornfeller's "private security" was primarily made up of out-of-work Special Forces, and included a few gun trucks, military helicopters and enough firepower to end the conflict tomorrow if we cared to. More than adequate for our purposes.

The bad news was it meant I didn't have many five-star meals in my future.

It appeared that the Munches returned to their most primitive instincts as they decayed, which meant a constant state of the double-H: horny and hungry. So we strapped the Munches we caught to treadmills and hung a fresh piece of meat or pornography in front them, and they'd march after them indefinitely without the slightest hint of frustration or fatigue.

Originally, my goal was to get enough zombies twirling their little hamster wheels to power a small home before I put them in front of the cameras; the wind power of tomorrow, that kind of thing. So far, the output was minimal, and it was looking like we'd have to fake it for now.

I noticed some of the Munches were missing limbs. That was expected, but one was missing a head.

"They don't need the heads?" I asked.

"The brain thing is apparently a myth," Mr. Devine said. "There's no 'soft spot,' so to speak."

"How far can you chop them down before they stop… living?" I asked.

"There's practically no limit," Devine said. "Whatever is powering them appears to be working on the cellular – possibly molecular -- level. "

That was incredible. "Is there any way to tap the energy source directly?"

"That depends on what the energy source is," Mr. Devine said. "It has to come from *somewhere*. I mean, if it doesn't, it flies in the face of everything we understand about not just physics but... pretty much anything. It would be like the bulk of human knowledge has turned out to be a big, elaborate illusion and we're starting all over again at zero. For a scientist... this is very troubling."

Right now, I was more concerned with getting everything ready to unveil to the press. "You keep on that."

* * * *

Tell me any three things about yourself, and I can tell you who you voted for in the last election. Tell me you prefer *American Idol* over *The Simpsons*, and I'll tell you your position on gun control. Tell me you eat Hostess Twinkies and own a plastic kiddy pool, and I can tell you if your father went to college. If you saw the latest Tarantino movie the day it opened and didn't buy anything from the concession stand, there's a four in five chance you fancy yourself an individualist. If you ordered the gummy worms, the odds increase to 95 percent.

If you have no idea who that is and own a sports utility vehicle, you check Fio's blog three point three times a day. If you prefer baseball to basketball you trust Fio more than the Washington Post.

That's why I do it. Because every time I make people believe what I tell them to, it confirms my understanding of human nature. That kind of power is intoxicating. Tell me any three things about you, and I can convince you of anything, absolutely anything – even if it's that the zombie apocalypse will save the planet.

Imagine what a rush that accomplishment would be.

* * * *

We broke the news on Fio's site so it would go unnoticed until we had whipped up his fan base. We needed them filling the comment sections as soon as the stories broke, calling and emailing journalists who drifted from the script.

For our first "glimpse" we used an unsteady iPhone video of a zombie stumbling into the Mitali wilderness, in homage to the famous Patterson-Gimlin Sasquatch film. The film was an inspiration to me. The same grainy uncertainty of the image that allowed skeptics to discount it was responsible for its allure. Not even capturing a Big Foot could compete with the interest generated by that film. It left just enough mystery to allow the mind to fill in the gaps. Once you had a specimen, it became but another uncovered species of primate, but the creature people saw in the Patterson-Gimlin film had been created in their own image. A real specimen was finite, the creature of the film one of infinite possibility.

I credit that film, more than anything else, with my decision to go into public relations.

* * * *

I worked Wayne Batton of CNC hard. Wayne was part of the old school, one of the last hold-outs against the fluctuating standards of new media and had managed to hang on by maintaining a loyal audience built up over the decades, which meant he had credibility – and nothing, and I mean nothing makes bullshit fly like credibility.

But I couldn't quite get him to bite, so I finally paid to fly out Calvin Aldridge, anchor for FNCtv, to Mitali. He arrived by helicopter gunship about the time the excitement had spread beyond Fio's followers to be noticed by cable news.

I greeted him at the heliport. I always had to brace myself for when I saw him without his cake makeup. The slowly degrading complexion had become increasingly difficult to cover-up with the rising frame rates and increasing resolution of home television.

"Sherry," he said, giving me a peck on the cheek in the European manner. "Thanks for giving me the scoop as always."

"I thought of you immediately," I said.

"Never bullshit a bullshitter," Aldridge said.

"I just hope you give us the same level of skepticism you gave the claims regarding my client from those scientists at the EPA, despite the clear conflict-of-interest I presented to you."

"I couldn't be the only one pushing that story. Perhaps if you had gotten some other nibbles, I could have discussed the fact that people were discussing it." He held me out at arm's length, gripping my shoulders as he looked me over the way the creepier old relatives greet their nieces. "You wouldn't have approached Batton first if credibility weren't important to you."

Aldridge took pride in his journalistic standards; the difference was Batton really had them.

"You know I wouldn't risk giving this to you if it wasn't 100 percent solid," I said. Batton was particularly susceptible to flattery.

"Let's see what you've got, then."

I gave him a tour of the facility and told him the current conflict was preparing to pack it up and abandon the operation until the outbreak changed his mind. "Fortunately, Hornfeller already had security on hand to round up as many zombies as we could before the situation spread."

"Out of patriotic duty?" Aldridge scoffed.

"We wouldn't turn away government assistance to offset the costs."

"It couldn't have come at a more opportune time, seeing as Hornfeller was under public pressure to abandon the facilities due to claims of human rights violations on the part of Hornfeller security."

Aldridge had done his homework. What he didn't know was that I was counting on it. "What would you have Hornfeller do? Hand the locals in his employ to the *genocidaires* at the gates who had come to haul them away to their deaths?"

This was actually true. What muddied the waters a bit was a case could be made the uprising was partially motivated by the perception one ethnic group had benefitted disproportionately from the nation's oil reserves. In addition to wiping out the Bindu, they had intended to reclaim the facility for themselves.

"Things are never cut-and-dry," Aldridge admitted. "When can I see these zombies?"

"Perpetual Terrorists," I corrected.

"As you like," he said.

I stopped before the lab doors. "I warn you, at first what you're going to see will be slightly disturbing, and could be easily misconstrued with a surface treatment – which is why I came to you," I lied. I took a beat then opened the door to a warehouse which had every square foot of floor space packed with the previously departed marching on treadmills like the world's largest fitness center.

"What the…"

"Now before you form any opinions, let me explain a few things. The Mitali government was in no position to deal with the outbreak. Mr. Hornfeller, recognizing the potential threat to humanity, was the only person in a place to do something about it. So he rounded up these bodies at great personal expense to contain the situation. For that the world owes Mr. Hornfeller a great debt of gratitude."

The horror on Aldridge's face had yet to fade. He covered his mouth with one hand, unable to speak.

"But it left him with a problem – what to do with all these animated beings once the threat of them being used as recyclable suicide bombers had been neutralized."

"It's insanity!" Aldridge said.

"Is it?" I motioned for the security guard to hand me his rifle and offered it to Aldridge, which made the guard uncomfortable. "Here. Go ahead. They're dead. Shoot one."

Aldridge stared down at the rifle, his expression softening.

"They may be dead, but we can't help but feel for them, can we? Our research shows them to have cognition slightly above brain death, but humans naturally empathize with the anthropomorphic. They look human, so we think of them as human.

"We could have simply locked them up in concentration camps, but that hardly seemed more humanitarian. We couldn't kill them, and we couldn't very well let them go, so what do you do?"

Aldridge didn't give an answer because he didn't have one.

"Look at him," I said, taking back the rifle. I handed it back to the guard and took a step closer to one of the machines where the Munch was strapped and bound except for his legs marching beneath him. "Does he look unhappy to you? Whatever is left of his previous existence, all he knows is the hunt for food. Eating does him no good, but the drive for basic needs is still there, so we give it to him. He is no less happy pursuing his prey here than he would be out there where people would die to fill a hunger that can never be satisfied. It was the only... humane thing to do."

Having nailed the pitch, I turned to look him in the eye to drive the last point home: "Look at him, Mr. Aldridge, and tell me one thing you would have differently."

Aldridge looked up at the former Bindu soldier, expressionless, locked in his eternal march.

"One," I asked again… but he couldn't.

* * * *

I wasn't called to the lab unless it was important. The whole gang was assembled, a statement in itself, including Mr. Hornfeller who had bothered to make the flight out, so they had something big for me.

"We found the energy source," Mr. Hornfeller beamed.

"How much do you know about quantum physics?" Mr. Hua asked.

"On a scale of one to ten? Zero," I said.

Mr. Devine stepped in. "All you need to know is it allows for an infinite number of universes existing independently of one another, and it appears when combined with our fuel additive cells we…," he stopped to glance at his *compadres* for moral support, "…well, as near as we can figure, draw this energy from other universes…"

"That's still unclear," Papa objected.

"The energy they're pulling appears to be what these other universes experience as the energy lost due to entropy. So energy isn't created or destroyed after all," Mr. Devine said, smiling. "I mean, it still violates everything we thought we understood about quantum mechanics, but some scientific principles remain intact, which is something."

"This is what allows the dead to continue, despite being unable to refuel?" I asked.

"In a manner of speaking, yes. It can go on, for all intents and purposes, forever. A perpetual motion machine, as it were."

"So these cells are able to draw upon energy essentially for free?"

Mr. Devine thought about it. "In a manner of speaking, yes."

"You said this was occurring on the molecular level?"

"That's right," Mr. Devine said.

That meant no only did we not need the heads, we didn't need their human forms at all. A relief since people tended to empathize with things that reminded them of the Munches previous living forms. "So we could grind them up into paste if wanted to?"

Mr. Hua seemed disturbed by the suggestion. "Theoretically, we could make a form of pink slime - although in this case it would be more of a phthalo/teal."

"Perfect," I accidentally thought aloud. I only wish I had known about this before I let Aldridge shoot all those rows of treadmills. His story could have been worse, but hit the main points I wanted emphasized. "Just don't call it Soylent Green," I said. On second thought… nope. Copyright issues.

"Green energy?" Mr. Hua offered.

I was a bit taken aback. I wasn't expecting it. "If Mr. Hornfeller didn't have you on the payroll, I'd hire you myself," I said. I liked it. I liked it a lot, but needed something to address the reanimation issue. "New Life," I said.

Their eyes softened as they played the name over in their heads.

"New Life Green Energy," I said, testing the lyricism of it.

I dialed. "Fio," I said when I heard his voice on the line. "Time to switch gears."

* * * *

"Calvin," I said, "you did such a bang-up job on the last story, I wanted to return the favor with an exclusive." I couldn't believe Batton passed on the story when we had a prototype battery, forcing me to go to Aldridge again.

There was some hesitation – that was the problem with Aldridge. He was automatically suspicious of anything Batton took a pass on, but no one pitched Aldridged unless Batton passed. But I eventually convinced him to do the follow-up with a promise of future scoops.

At first, we confined our sale of New Life vehicles to Mitali, which, still healing from a brutal war, was desperate for any economic boost. Experiencing actual death didn't give them the luxury of abstractions like honoring the dead.

A black market quickly sprouted up for rich with nothing left to buy but novelty items. The use of Mitali corpses gave enough wiggle room to sell a few to Korea and other third world dictatorships. It wasn't long before we had drained the graveyards of Mitali dry and were going to need fresh meat.

"It's time," I announced at our monthly meeting.

Our operation couldn't grow without generating new fuel, which meant expanding our reach beyond the borders of Mitali. We couldn't go global until we came clean about what had ultimately been responsible for the reanimation.

Mr. Hornfeller, long accustomed to my maneuvering any misgivings, didn't look concerned. "You think we can manage it?"

"Yeah," I said, without my usual level of confidence. "It's going to require some major finessing, but yeah. I do."

* * * *

This time, Batton nibbled, but the tip didn't come from me, but a whistleblower in our organization. She had been causing problems, so we forged a document detailing all of Hornfeller's as-yet-unexposed sins, but left enough inconsistencies in the official letterhead to expose the "fraud" on Fio's blog within hours of his report to get the chattering class debating the authenticity rather than the contents.

18

In the ensuing fallout, we called for Batton's resignation if the network wanted to avoid a massive libel suit.

I made an exception and met Fio in person at a local bar to watch Batton's resignation and swap shots of mescal. Now that Batton's head had rolled, the whole topic would be too radioactive for other journalists to touch.

"That's what you get for making me go to Aldridge," I said, toasting the TV.

The truth would come out, but in drips and dribbles. By the time commentators could openly admit the contents of the document were, in fact, accurate, the public would have already become accustomed to the idea.

We'd have to make good use of our earned period of immunity. Due to their unique combination of capitalism and authoritarian communist regime, China would be the perfect proving ground for a global push. The rest of the world, beset with increasing damage to highly populated coastal areas from rising waters and severe weather were happy to look the other way if the most populous nation on Earth decided to switch to a carbon neutral technology. Once we got a foothold in China, it would be onward to India, then, eventually, Europe.

"Mind if I ask you serious question?" Fio asked.

"A serious one? I'm not sure I can handle that."

He stared at the TV, the glow of the screen lighting up the five days of stubble on his face like a moonlit forest. "How do you know when the job is finished?"

I had to think about it for a few moments before I formulated an answer. "This contract will end the way any contract ends: the client stops paying, or I retire."

"What would you need to achieve before you could retire?"

I finished my drink. "Not sure. It would have to be pretty big, though, to satisfy me."

"This is big," Fio said. "At least for me."

I put a hand on his shoulder. "Don't retire on me, yet. We've only touched the surface of what we can do."

* * * *

Globalization had allowed me to move back to the States, so I now held our monthly meetings at Hornfeller's ranch in Texas.

Mr. Hua was concerned about the groups that had organized as additive's connection to New Life technology sunk in, but were still largely viewed as whackos.

"Doesn't matter," I said. Hua didn't' seem to believe me, so I handed him my pad with the browser opened to this morning's news story. "CO_2 levels were leveling off – and Hornfeller was responsible," I said. The world was now officially dependent, even if they didn't know it, yet. "We hold the trump card."

"What's that?" Mr. Papa asked.

I smiled. I couldn't help it. "The patent. We're officially too big to fail."

"There's only one thing left to do," Mr. Hornfeller said.

"What's that?" I asked.

"No product could be said to have made it until it made it in the States."

He was right. If I were to wrap things up now, it would still feel like a job half done. We needed to take the States. I wouldn't be content merely releasing the New Life vehicles into the marketplace, either; I would only be satisfied if I had the public on board to the point they'd put their own grandmothers in the gas tank. Do that, and I really could retire.

* * * *

Fio bought an island in 2030 and devoted his time to writing science fiction. I continued working after Hornfeller and I parted ways because I wouldn't know what to do with myself otherwise. Did I feel like I left the job half finished?

There was a time I would have said no. We had converted entirely to a Green Energy-based economy. Most people now opted for "cold cremation" as the cleaner alternative, and we ran a successful advertising campaign to position the contributing of one's body to stem the tides, quite literally, of global warming as the equivalent of organ donation.

I did scale back my hours and became more selective about my clients. I made sure the firm could run without me as I slowly transitioned to a more ceremonial role of hosting seminars and speaking at fundraisers.

My first taste of doubt would occur when Hornfeller, Jr. paid me a visit. He was in better shape than his father; good-looking, like he had the potential to age well.

"I was sorry to hear about your father," I said. From what I read, he had assumed the day-to-day operations of New Life.

"Yes. That's actually why I'm here," he said. "I have a straight promotional job for you." He raised his hands before I had a chance to object, "I know you usually find promotion beneath you, but in this case, I can think of no one else who should handle it."

"I'm listening."

"Were you aware that my father was originally a British citizen?"

"I was," I said. "Your father and I worked together for many years."

"He always spoke of how integral you were to his company's success. Which is why I thought you should share the honor. It's been decided he should be laid to rest at Westminster Abbey." Hornfeller, Jr. smiled proudly.

For the first time in my career, I didn't know what to say.

Junior laughed. "You heard me right. Isaac Newton, Charles Darwin and Antony Hornfeller."

"Is this a joke?" There was simply no way to spin this one.

"The church feels, considering what he's done," Junior said.

"He didn't do anything," I snorted.

Junior's face slackened. "My father was a great man."

I couldn't believe what I was hearing. "Your father was a con man – like me!"

"The world was hurtling towards destruction… if New Life Energy hadn't come along…"

"Do you know why your father chose to be buried rather than 'cold cremated?'" I asked. "Did you ever stop to ask yourself why, after all the people he's convinced to do it, he would choose not to?" Keeping that hidden from the public was one of my bigger achievements.

Hornfeller, Jr. clasped his hands behind him. "No."

"Because it's bullshit! Don't you see? You father came up with it in a brainstorming session one night to save his ass after toxic waste… it was a human atrocity, and we had to massage it. He was there. So he knows no sane person would subject themselves to such a process. Not without years of work on my part."

"Even if what you say were true, it doesn't change things."

"What are you talking about? It changes everything!"

"Did we, or did we not stop global warming?" he asked.

I didn't know how to answer that. "I suppose, in a way, it was clean, and renewable... which is why we chose to message it that way…" Hornfeller, Jr. smiled haughtily. "I don't have to explain it to you," I snapped. "I was there!"

22

"So what? However the two of you came up with it, New Energy stopped a world crisis. Protest all you want, Ms. Constantine, you and my father saved us."

"But…," I said. "But," I started again…

"I really thought you'd be happy about this," he said.

"Happy?" I said in disbelief. "Why on Earth would I be happy about this?"

"Why should you be happy to be honored for your achievements?" he asked, getting flustered.

"You don't get buried at Westminster Abbey unless you've really done something great. Something wonderful. Newton, Darwin – those are great men! If they bury your father there, then what have I achieved?"

"I'm afraid I don't know how to answer that," he said. "It seems to say you've achieved quite a lot.

"How?" This whole conversation was driving me crazy. "If all this crap about clean energy and saving the environment is true – don't you see what you're saying?"

"I'm saying you're a great woman!" Hornfeller, Jr. said. This time he was the one shouting.

"You're saying New Energy isn't a fraud! And if it's not a fraud, then I *am*," I said, poking my chest with my finger. "Don't you see? If New Energy is really as great as you say it is…. Why, then, you didn't need me at all! A product like that could have sold itself!"

Zero Hour
by Derek Muk

Jamie turned the key, trying to start the engine of the 1973 Mercury Capri. Nothing happened at first, no noise or anything. When she tried again there was a dying whine, like the sound of an animal on its last legs that emitted from the engine.

She looked at Henry, sitting next to her in the passenger seat. He was a young, handsome black man with a modest afro. The interior of the vehicle reeked of his aftershave.

"Whoops, that doesn't sound promising!" she quipped.

Henry's dark brow furrowed. "Hold on," he replied and went back out to take a look under the hood again. After making a few adjustments, he said, "Okay, try it again."

Jamie turned the key but heard the same melancholic whine from the engine. "Shoot," she said under her breath. *Hope Henry's not selling me a lemon! He wouldn't do that, he's a good friend. . .thing's like this just happen.* She was in her mid-twenties, athletic build, raking her hand through her short dark brown hair. People told her she resembled the actress, Kate Jackson. She always smiled when they said that, accepting that as a compliment.

He was still poking under the hood, performing his magic. And magician he definitely is! He had helped her out so many times, pulling her out of jams with her laptop, her previous car, her hi-fi stereo system, and even a laundry machine at her former house. He was a real jack-of-all-trades. She lost track of how many times she said to him, '*I owe you one!*'

"Start her up!" Henry bellowed, breaking her out of her nostalgia and back into the present.

She obeyed, and this time to her relief, the Capri's engine roared to life! She broke out a relieved smile. She stepped on the gas pedal when he told her to. After he dropped the hood he sat next to her again inside the car, pushing his big '70s-style glasses up his nose.

Henry grinned. "That's another one you *owe* me, Lady Cyclone."

"You're psychic! You read my mind!" she jabbed sarcastically. "Put it on my tab!"

"Can we be '*friends with benefits*' and call it even?"

She punched him playfully in the arm. "I'm gonna kill you!"

* * * *

Jamie got to her class early that evening. Before closing the door of her new Capri (well, technically, it wasn't *new*) she caught another whiff of Henry's aftershave from inside. Man, it was strong! She took one more admirable look at the dark green car before trotting off to the cafeteria. She smiled, feeling good and confident that the sporty little car was hers now. *Yes! A cool car for the new year,* she mused. She was glad she was able to grab some tea at the cafeteria before they closed. When she arrived at the classroom, sipping her tea, a few other students were already there, immersed in their textbooks. One of these students, an Asian man, in his forties roughly, with shaggy black hair and a bushy mustache and beard, closed his book and looked at a bright orange flyer.

Jamie sat at a desk near him. "Hey, I saw one of those on the school bulletin board," she commented, hoping she wasn't disturbing him.

He turned to her, shooting her a friendly smile. "A guy was passing them around outside the library." He shifted his glasses up his nose. "'*Are you prepared for Doomsday? Are you ready for Judgment Day? Discover what the government's hiding from you!*'" he read aloud in a deep, ominous tone of voice.

She smiled. "Hey, good radio voice. Might I be sitting next to the next Orson Welles?"

He laughed. "I wish! Still, there's something about this that I'm curious about."

Jamie sipped some more tea. "Interesting it's related to what we're studying, huh?"

"Yeah. Boy, the reading in the Bowen book sure raised my eyebrows, about all those contagious diseases and how they can zap you into a zombie. The government and the military are testing some serious stuff and the worst part about it is that they aren't telling us anything. That's pathetic!"

"*They're* pathetic," she chided.

"Did you write the paper yet?"

"Nope. I've been so bad, procrastinating like hell." She lowered her voice to a whisper. "Don't tell anyone but I've been dabbling more on my art collage projects than my homework. And on top of all that there's my job and roller derby. So I don't have a whole lot of time, you know?"

"Wow, roller derby, huh? Sounds fun."

She took off her hooded sweat jacket and showed him a dark bruise on her arm. "It's not when you get these. But I won't complain too much. I get an adrenaline rush out of it, that's what matters."

He nodded. "Cool. Oh, my name's David, by the way."

"Jamie," she replied, shaking his hand firmly. "Nice talkin' to you." Just then the teacher stepped in and people got to their seats. Jamie nodded at the bright orange flyer. "Say, would you like to attend that lecture together?"

"Sure."

* * * *

On Wednesday night Jamie and her fellow teammates battled it out with their arch rivals, the Cougars, at the roller derby ring in the Cougars' hometown of Concord, Ca. Competing before a packed, enthusiastic crowd, Jamie was involved in a few key moves and plays that ultimately crowned her and her fellow Cyclones with a victory. A banner hanging above the scoreboard read: **'The Annual California State Roller Derby Finals'**

The remaining seconds on the scoreboard winded down to zero and a gun was fired, making it official. Jamie, her Cyclones jersey drenched in sweat, beamed and hugged her teammates excitedly. Her teammates and coach kept chanting, "Jamie, Jamie, Jamie!" She was the hero for the day and enjoyed every minute of it. After the awards ceremony where their coach was handed the coveted trophy of the finals, the team headed for the locker room. Jamie took a nice, warm shower, letting the soothing spray of water massage her body. When she was finished she dried herself and threw on a jersey with the Rolling Stones' iconic tongue logo on it, pulled on a pair of tight blue jeans, and slipped into some canvas sneakers.

After hugging her teammates goodnight she jumped into her Capri, inserted the key, and turned. . .only to hear the dreaded dying whine once more. *Oh, shoot!!* She tried to start the engine again and it choked up the same sound in response. Sighing, she whipped out her cell phone and hit the button for Henry's number.

Henry came all the way to the dark, nearly deserted parking lot of the roller derby ring in Concord. One of her teammates kept her company while he was on his way. With Jamie holding up a powerful flashlight Henry tinkered around under the hood for a while. When he was done, his hands and clothing smudged with grease, he said: "Okay, start her up."

She turned the key and the Capri roared to life. Like it had clawed itself back from the dead. "Yes!" she smiled. "You're a genius!"

Before she could open her mouth again, he looked her dead in the eye with a mischievous grin. "Don't say it. You *owe* me one, Lady Cyclone!"

* * * *

The next evening, Jamie met David at Contra Costa College. The campus was unusually quiet. Hallways were empty, the library that was typically full had only a handful of people inside, and the parking lot was mostly vacant. As she approached David she saw that he was reading the Bowen textbook, squinting at times.

"Reading under fluorescents is bad for your eyes," Jamie said.

"Oh, hi." He closed the book. "I know. Bad habit. How are you?"

"Glad it's not a school night."

"Tell me about it! So, acquire any more bruises since our last class?"

"As a matter of fact, yes. We won the finals last night. Off to the championships! Yoo-hoo!"

"Hey, congratulations!"

"Thanks. Still haven't started that darn paper!"

"You're not the only one," he replied consolingly. He opened the door to the social sciences building and they went into an amphitheater-type classroom where the seats looked down at a stage below. A couple of people were sitting in the front. Jamie and David sat in the middle.

Moments later, an African American woman with a big, poofy afro stepped onto the stage. She was joined by another woman dressed all in black. After the classroom filled up with more attendees the woman with the afro cleared her throat and said into a microphone: "Good evening, ladies and gentlemen. Thanks for coming out. My name's Billy and this here is Lucy. We came tonight to inform you, educate you about what our government and the U.S. military are hiding from you, about what they don't want you to know." She looked at members of the audience. "Some of you told me earlier that you caught the really graphic, disturbing You Tube video with the U.S. military scientists experimenting and torturing some poor Iraqi man."

"They pulled the video off," a man in the crowd said.

Billy shook her head disgustedly. "Hmmm, I'm not surprised. See, now they're gonna start censoring everything, closing websites and links, editing news reports. Well, it ain't nothin' new, people, so don't look surprised. We've been in a military state for too long. From them being able to track all of our cell phone calls, pinpoint where we are physically and on the web. Hey, it's a miracle that I'm even allowed to speak on this very stage. But anything can happen. We may lose freedom of speech tomorrow."

Jamie turned to David, whispering: "Did you see the footage?"

He shook his head.

"In that video a man was drugged, had every right stripped away from him, and basically served as a human guinea pig for these scientists' sadistic, morbid curiosity," Billy continued. "They poked needles into him, sliced him up, ripped organs from his body without his consent, and tested him under extreme, inhuman

conditions with dangerous viruses, bugs, toxins, and chemicals."
Someone in the audience gasped. "Yeah, tell me about it! But this
ain't nothin' new, folks. Been happenin' a long time, the
government just knows how to cover it up, that's all."

"Bush is to blame!" a woman shouted.

"Oh, he ain't the only one, sista," Billy replied into the
microphone. "You know what happened to that poor Iraqi man?
The video keeps it sweet and short, not revealing. . .he basically
turned into some biological war machine for our dear military."
Billy nodded. "Yep. Uncle Sam won't tell you that but us folks
underground have our ears pressed to the ground."

"Where is he now?" Jamie asked.

Billy looked at her. "Good question." She clicked her
laptop's mouse and a picture popped up on the white projection
screen. Everyone gasped. It showed a man with a scarred,
disfigured face, with a mismatched nose and pair of lips that had
been stitched on hastily. One of his oversized ears was hanging on
by a few stitches. He had blonde hair and did not look Middle
Eastern in origin. His eyes had a glazed, glaucoma type film over
them. Billy clicked the mouse again and another photo showed the
man, dressed in combat attire, shuffling around in the desert with a
limp.

"He's a zombie!" Jamie exclaimed.

Billy looked at her again. "Exactly. Helping us kill his
former fellow countrymen. And you know what, people? He did
not consent to this. All his rights were stripped away. Somewhere,
his family, his wife is out there not knowing what became of him.
And now, it's up to us to destroy these zombies. It's the
government's problem, their creation but they ain't doing squat."

"So you're saying there are zombies here, too?" David
asked.

"Yes. And their numbers are growing, people. Somehow,
someway some of them escaped from the U.S. military's research
laboratories and they've been infecting and killing other humans."

"How come I haven't read or seen anything on the news about this?" Jamie asked.

"Like I said, it's a massive cover up, sista," Billy answered. "Now I think it's time to chat strategies on how to fight these creatures. Who's with me now?"

Some people walked out quietly. "Hey, this is a democracy, but it's your future, too." She looked at the remaining audience members. "Are you prepared to fight injustice with justice, people?"

Jamie and David looked at one another. "I gotta tell my buddy, Al, about this," she mused excitedly.

"Who's he?" David inquired curiously.

"Oh, he's an anthropology professor at UC Berkeley that's into weird, kooky paranormal stuff like this. Wait till he hears about this. Wonder if he saw that video?"

* * * *

Jamie called Albert Taylor's number numerous times but he never picked up. Later she learned from his supervisor, Russ, that Al was away on an 'investigation.' Russ and her chatted for a bit and he told her that he saw the You Tube vid too before it was removed. The national championship was today but her mind was preoccupied with those freaky zombie photos Billy showed as well as thoughts about the end of the world. She surfed the Internet for articles related to the Contra Costa College lecture but nothing surfaced. Maybe Billy was right, looked like the government had wiped out all data on the topic.

She grabbed her roller skates and jumped into her 1973 Mercury Capri that still reeked of Henry's aftershave. Jeez, that stuff was potent! She opened all the windows and zoomed off. At a red light the Capri's engine died and she panicked. Luckily, she was able to restart the car and floored the gas pedal. *I'm gonna kill that Henry!!* She trusted him when he sold the Capri to her. Fortunately, the car made it all the way to Sacramento without any problems. When she reached the roller derby ring she dressed up in the locker room and hit the floor.

However, throughout the competition she found herself easily distracted by those grotesque zombie images again. One time she got elbowed hard by a rival team member and skidded to the ground. But she was reenergized by a second wind and helped contribute some strong key plays that catapulted the Cyclones to a championship win. Her fellow teammates carried her out of the ring on their shoulders like she was a sacred queen.

David and her were studying one night at the CCC library when she whispered to him: "I got a message from Billy. There's been a zombie sighting."

He looked intrigued, closing his textbook. "Where?"

"C'mon, I'll brief you on the way." They got in her Capri and drove to downtown Richmond near the Amtrak station, where along a dark, deserted stretch of tracks, they spotted two hulking figures shambling around. David pointed a flashlight at them and they both groaned, flashing rotted teeth and torn lips. One was wearing a combat uniform.

"One's fresh off the press from the military's research facilities," David muttered.

Suddenly, Billy appeared out of nowhere at Jamie's driver side window and she jumped.

"Sorry!" Billy whispered. "Didn't mean to scare you." She ran her fingers through her big afro. "I've got weapons, people. Park your car and follow me."

Jamie parked the vehicle near a warehouse and she and David trailed Billy to a dark van near the railroad tracks. Billy opened the sliding door of the van and handed each of them a gun.

"I don't know how to use this!" Jamie said.

"Trust me, it ain't that difficult," Billy replied, giving them a quick, basic lesson on firearms. "You'll get the hang of it.

Oh, I did a little research on you, sista." She grinned. "If you can slam some chick in roller derby this will be a piece of cake for you."

Billy looked at David. "Do you have any special talents? I didn't find any."

He chuckled. "You did well. I'm actually that boring in real life."

"They're coming!" Billy nodded at the two shuffling zombies. When they got closer she aimed a handgun at the head of the one in the combat uniform and squeezed the trigger. Its head exploded like a watermelon and it collapsed to the ground. She shot the other creature in the forehead, too. "Remember, people, always aim for their heads. That's how you kill the suckers."

"Zombie 101," David commented. "Nice. Where's your group?"

"You're basically looking at it. My other buddies couldn't make it tonight."

"Where'd you get this arsenal?" Jamie asked.

"Hobby of mine. Shhh!" she whispered. "Dead ahead!"

David and Jamie looked at what she was viewing, seeing a quartet of the living dead shambling their way along the train tracks. As they got closer, Billy shined a flashlight at them and they saw another zombie dressed in combat attire. Bloodstains smeared its uniform and one of its ears was dangling by a thread of flesh. A female zombie limping next to it wore a housedress with tacky floral designs on it.

Billy smiled at Jamie and said, "You do the honors, Miss roller derby."

Jamie aimed the gun carefully at the soldier's head and fired. She missed it by inches and the monster groaned, lumbering towards them. "Damn! Now I got it pissed off!" She aimed and fired again and this time the bullet hammered the soldier's forehead.

"Good job!" Billy said. She and David helped her finish off the rest of the creatures.

"So how come the government hasn't quarantined any of these things?" Jamie inquired, parting back her short dark brown hair with her hand.

"Remember what I said back at the lecture now, sista," Billy reminded. "It's all a cover up. If they're caught with one then people will know they're at fault, will start questioning. The less they do they're happy."

Jamie nodded. "Have you networked with other resistance groups?"

"Trying to but a lot of folks are scared, understandably so. And they ain't talkin' much, you dig? Which is why I held that lecture, to make contact with others."

They returned to Jamie's Mercury Capri. "Well, thanks for your help, people," Billy smiled. "Much obliged to ya. I'll holla at chu again when there's another sighting."

* * * *

At work Jamie surfed the Internet for any zombie news but found zilch. *Government removed all links about the topic?* She wondered. She still couldn't believe that she killed some zombies!! Wow! Who'd believe her? So she was a murderer. She deserved to be thrown in prison, right? But technically, the victims were already dead and they had posed a dangerous threat to humans. When her shift was over she went home and forced herself to start her paper for class, easily distracted by her art collage project as well as the television and her hi-fi stereo system. She threw a record on the turntable and soon Foreigner's "Cold as Ice" blared from the speakers.

Midway into the song her phone rang. She answered it after the third ring. "Hello?"

"It's showtime again, sista," Billy greeted. "Meet me at the Richmond Army substation in fifteen minutes. Oh, and can you pick up David at his apartment? He doesn't have a car." Then the line clicked dead. Hey, what was she? One of her henchmen now?!

Jamie turned off the stereo and left.

After she picked up David, she drove to the Army substation on Carlson Boulevard. The skies were already dark and the trio turned on their flashlights as they approached a fence. Billy pointed ahead. On the other side, hidden among a maze of military trucks and jeeps were a group of zombies. Jamie saw another one that was in a soldier's uniform, a machine gun slung across his chest. They carefully climbed over the barbed wire fence and quickly ran for cover behind a truck. Cradled in Billy's arms was a shotgun. She was dressed all in black. David gripped a handgun and Jamie also had a shotgun, trying not to appear awkward with it.

"You look brave tonight, sista," Billy smiled. Her pearly white teeth shined under the moonlight. "Be my guest."

Jamie felt like rolling her eyes but refrained. Instead, she took a deep breath, aimed the shotgun carefully at the zombie soldier, and squeezed the trigger. The bullet missed, striking the side of a truck and she cursed under her breath. "Shows you what an expert marksman I am," she whispered sarcastically.

The creatures were already shuffling their way, groaning in vengeance. Jamie aimed the weapon at the soldier again and this time the bullet hit its chest. As it limped closer, she aimed and fired once more, this time hitting the bull's eye target of its forehead. It crumpled to the ground. The other creatures converged upon them, kicking their fallen comrade out of the way. Nothing would stand in their way to get human flesh.

David stepped forward, aimed his handgun, and fired, bringing down a black zombie that was dressed in a fireman's uniform.

"Good shot!" Billy praised. She herself shot down three of the creatures.

One of the zombies quickly shambled over to David, almost taking a chunk out of his neck. But Jamie's fast reflexes prompted her to intervene in time and she swung the shotgun's butt viciously at the creature's head, over and over until it fell to the ground. Then she hastily shot it in the head.

"Thanks!" he sighed. "Whoa! That was close!"

Suddenly, they were surrounded by an army of the walking dead in the middle of the huge parking lot. Some of them groaned, some had their arms raised forward as they walked.

"Jesus!" Jamie whispered, her big brown eyes widening. "Where'd they come from?!"

"This way!" Billy said, leading them through a narrow gap between two creatures.

As they were running Jamie whipped out her cell phone and called Henry. *He's gonna kill me. It's late and he'll think I want another favor*, she thought. He took the words straight out of her mouth when he answered.

"Want another favor, huh, Lady Cyclone?" he asked sarcastically. "What? Car broke down again?"

"No, this is different," Jamie replied sheepishly. "Well, sort of. My friends and I are in a bit of a jam right now and wondered if you can help us."

"Jamie, Jamie, Jamie," he said, chuckling. "What would you do without me? Where you at, girl?"

* * * *

Henry arrived twelve minutes later, wearing a New Orleans Saints jersey and semi-baggy jeans. After Jamie introduced him to everyone, Billy grinned and nodded approvingly.

"You did well, sista," she said, eyeing Henry's stocky frame from head to toe. "Never figured you to have a thing with a brotha. But never judge a book by its cover, right?"

"We're just friends," Jamie added.

"Sure, that's what they all say," Billy laughed.

Henry laughed, too, until he looked at Jamie. "So you said something about 'zombies'? Now did I hear you correctly or was it just wax in my ears?"

She looked him straight in the eye. "Zombies, Henry, like in the movies. Only they're real!"

Henry looked at Billy. "Has she been smoking something?"

"She's tellin' the truth, brotha," Billy said. They were hiding inside an empty warehouse in the substation, trying to buy some time. She gave him the skinny on the whole government cover up affair.

Henry raised his eyebrows. "Wow!"

"You're a cop but you didn't hear anything about this?" David asked.

"Naw, man, this is all new to me."

"Now we gotta figure a way out of here," Billy said. "They're all over the substation."

"Lemme see if I can get some backup from my boys," Henry interjected, taking his cell phone out. He frowned when he looked at the screen. "Aw, shoot! I ain't got no bars!"

The rest of the group checked their phones, too, and noticed the same thing.

Henry brought his gun out, making sure it was loaded. "We're gonna have to fight our way outta here then." He looked at Jamie, shaking his head disapprovingly. "What kinda mess did you drag me into, Lady Cyclone?"

Her big brown eyes looked away sheepishly. "Sorry, Henry," she muttered.

"You're gonna *owe* me big time for this one, you hear?"

Billy looked out the window of the warehouse at the growing number of zombies. It was like watching an army of ants coming out of an anthill. The moonlight danced across her chocolate brown face. She raked her hand through her big, poofy afro, turning to Henry. "I like your idea, man. Let's make a break for it. Run through that gauntlet of stinkin' corpses for the fence on the other side of the parking lot."

"Sounds like suicide," David retorted, shifting his glasses up his nose.

"You have any better ideas?" Billy snapped. "We're faster than them, that's for sure."

Jamie rubbed her chin in thought. "My vote is for us to stay put here until they go away. I mean, if they don't find us they'll wander to someplace else to get food, right?"

Henry checked his cell phone again, frowning, "Still no network."

Jamie wondered if the government was responsible for their phones being out or if this area was just a dead zone.

"Could be waitin' forever, sista," Billy remarked.

Henry looked at Jamie. "C'mon, Lady Cyclone, let's split. She's right. We're faster than those guys. C'mon, you'll whiz by them like the way you do on your roller skates. By the way, congrats on winning the championship."

Jamie managed a weak grin. "Thanks. . .okay, I'm in."
David threw in his vote, agreeing with her.

* * * *

They left the warehouse, running under the full moon. As they rounded a corner, an obese zombie wearing stained overalls lunged out of the darkness and grabbed Henry, knocking the gun out of his hand. The creature coughed, spraying green phlegm and mucous all over Henry's face. "Oh, God!" he scowled.

David shot the creature in the head and it plopped to the ground. Henry quickly wiped the green liquid from his face. The quartet moved on, cautious whenever they approached pitch black niches and spaces. Jamie took the lead, running and dodging zombies, trying to reach that fence on the other side of the lot. She felt like she was on the roller derby ring, knocking, shoving, and pushing bodies out of her way. She elbowed a monster out of her path, imagining it to be a rival opponent. Her body was still sore from the beating she endured in the championship. She got so absorbed in her goal of trying to get to that fence that she forgot about the others. When she looked over her shoulder the only person she saw was Billy.

They arrived at a clearing, free of the creatures. "Where's Henry and David?" Jamie panted, catching her breath. She scanned the dark, shadowy landscape but saw nothing but shuffling black figures. As her eyes adjusted better to the night she turned a little to her right, her jaw dropping open. For there, squatting beside an Army jeep was Henry, bloody flesh dripping from his mouth! And the body he was feasting off of was David's! When Henry finally saw her staring at him his blood shot eyes bulged out even more. There was a ravenous sickness in those eyes, a look of sheer madness. Jamie and Billy started back pedaling when Henry got up and headed their way. Jamie couldn't take her eyes off his pale, deathly face, at the transformation.

Her eyes got watery. "Henry!" she called out, hoping 'he' could still hear her, that his soul was still intact. "Noooooooooooo!" When she started going towards him Billy grabbed her arm and yanked her in the direction of the fence.

"It's too late, sista," Billy reasoned. They were getting closer. Billy fired her shotgun at a bunch of the living dead that were cornering them against the fence. Heads exploded. Henry was the last one among the group.

Billy didn't say anything, just gave her some space. With her teary big brown eyes, Jamie took a deep breath before aiming her shotgun at his deathly face and fired. Then she dropped the weapon and leaned against the fence, crying.

Billy hugged her gently. "I'm sorry," she whispered. After a moment, she gave Jamie a boost up the fence.

Prisoners of Forever
by Katie Jones

It's hard to sleep at night, when your nightmares now walk the earth. The memories of the old world seem like centuries ago, torn to shreds by the cold hard reality of this new strange land. A human being on this earth can feel so far away from home, or what was once home. The loneliness is profound and consumes all that is left of the human spirit. At times it feels as though you are the last person alive, all other forms of life are just forms of imagination, ghosts and phantoms of things that once existed. Or perhaps, you are the ghost haunting a new world.

This is how the young woman felt as she sat inside a small, rundown cottage; thick, rusted bars covered the windows, allowing her to see the sun as it began to set, spilling crimson colors into the sky outside. But the woman inside could not focus on the brilliant colors flooding the sky above, she was too busy securing the run down shack she now called home, and had been calling home for months now. It was a small, wooden place on the outskirts of the remote outback, sand and dust settled in every nook and cranny, and she worked hard to pull the blinds down over the windows, an attempt to keep out the darkness and everything that lived in those shadows.

But before she could settle down for the night, she had to check the perimeter outside. She hid tears behind a warriors face, she wasn't old, no more than 26 years but she felt ancient, she had seen things no one should ever have to witness. Her hair was cut short, shorn with blunt, rust colored scissors she'd found outside. Her clothes were worn, a once white shirt now the color of red mud, and her cutoff jeans were ripped, faded and stained, they hung off her emaciated body like loose fabric, her protruding hipbones poked out from underneath the fabric, a sign of just how bad things really were.

She opened the old, wooden door as silently as she could but nevertheless a slight creak filled the still night, and she reached for her shot gun, before she slung it over her tiny shoulder as she moved out, well-worn boots stepping into the dirt outside. This was her home, her world, a small acre of arid, desert land situated in the heart of Australia, surrounded by wire she'd scrounged up over the years.

The fence was at least seven feet high, created by mismatched bits of fences, wire and tin she'd stumbled upon over time, but she knew she had to ensure it would stay secure. And so she moved towards the perimeter, slowly and silently, her eyes scanned the shadows as daylight began to dim. In places she'd covered up holes with odd bits of tin, and secured it down with whatever she could find. But as she made her way around the small rectangle of land, she could see them coming in the distance.

Three of them, they moved together and walked slowly towards the side of the fence where she was. She crouched down and watched, their jerking movements, but they didn't unsettle her anymore, nor did the odd gurgles, growls and groans they emitted. The decaying flesh that clung to their bones was unsightly, even after all these years, but this wasn't what bothered her. What

44

bothered her most was the stench, like rotten meat that wafted into the air and filled her lungs, by now her gag reflex didn't budge at this smell, but it still made her uneasy.

These creatures made a beeline towards the fence, and once they got there, they stumbled into it, pressing their swollen fingers to the gaps and trying to grip at the woman behind it. The female monster pressed her disfigured face into the wire; the rotten globe of her eyeball bulged against it and oozed black colored mucus. The males were less aggressive, some might call them gentlemen compared to the female, they stood behind her waiting, but the flaring nostrils gave away their true desires as the caught the scent of a living human.

She didn't have to shoot them, they were the only ones as far as her eyes could see, the thought that they were here made her edgy. She knew she should keep the ammunition. And so she walked on, and ignored the creatures as they stumbled and followed her around. The constant scrape of dead weight irritated her as they dragged their feet, losing footing whenever a jagged, protruding bone caught onto a rock beneath them.

Eventually the woman went back inside, and the creatures continued to push monotonously at the fence, rotten teeth gnawing at wire until they chipped and broke. The woman entered her house and bolted the door and before she settled down in a corner of the shack, on an old, grey woolen blanket, she used a knife to force open a rusted can, and began to scoop the contents of baked beans into her mouth with her fingers. She chewed slowly, and used her tongue to lick at the juices sliding down her hand. Once finished, she curled into a fetal position and rested on the floor, eye lids half closed, unable to allow herself to fall fully asleep.

The woman went by the name, Birdie, it wasn't her real name, but it was something she'd picked up when she was a teenager, living on the streets of a city almost as deadly as this new world. These days she was thankful to have been a street kid, she knew in her heart that if she had lived an easy life she would be dead and walking around like those things outside. Back in the old days there were others like her and she would stumble across them frequently, but once the dead stopped dying and humans became rare, she knew the safest place was to get away from all of humanity, well, what was left of it. The jeep she'd stolen on her escape brought her to the remote outback, and she still had it here with her, it sat outside, like a trusty old friend.

Sometimes she would have to leave this sanctuary, drive north to the old towns that used to house others, siphon what fuel she could get and collect food as she went. But the trips had become longer and longer, she had to travel further than before just to survive. And going out there was beyond dangerous.

The flickering light of dawn woke her from a tormented, troubled sleep. And Birdie rubbed her eyes, she stumbled towards the window and peered out through the blind. She couldn't see them. With some relief flooding her, she moved towards a barrel and sipped at the water, cupping it in her hands and washing the grime off her face. Today she had to go out. And with dread in her heart, she prepared herself.

Birdie took the shot gun, as well as a small revolver and a back pack filled with little more than a water bottle. She needed the room to carry what she could find. She found her way to the rust colored Jeep, she opened the door and turned on the ignition, the familiar rumble of the engine comforted her, and this old vehicle seemed like her only friend in this cruel, isolated world. The petrol fumes rose high into the polluted sky above her, black smoke billowing out of the exhaust pipe. In the corner of her eye she spotted those creatures from last night, moving towards the fence. With a sigh she left the jeep and ran before she took out the shot gun and walked towards them, her eyes locked onto the female and Birdie took in the skinny, dead girl with lifeless, sunken eyes and black, matted hair. She shot this one in the face, and the front of its skull exploded, causing the creature to fall to its knees, fingers moving through the earth and gripping at the ground as the black goo inside of its head splattered across the red dirt. The others were next, and she planted bullets strait into their decomposing brains, this released the soup within their skulls with a splatter that soaked the soil at her feet.

Once, the dead stayed dead, enzymes and bacteria within the body caused the dead to decay and bloat. These would then eat away at the membranes and walls dividing the insides and cause them to become nothing but a soup, which sloshed around in a silent, vessel. This was no longer the case because even though they were falling to bits, these things would not stay dead.

Birdie, sighed, finally she unlocked the padlock that secured the chains, and pushed open the gate, drove through, fastened the gate again and sped off down the dirt road.

The summer heat was suffocating at times, since the earth had become so polluted, temperatures had risen. But Birdie didn't turn on the air conditioner, luxuries like this were a thing of the past, fuel consumption came first, and she had to save every last drop in the tank. She drove for about an hour before Birdie pulled up into a ghost town; it consisted of nothing more than a few houses, a petrol station and a shop. There was zilch here because she had taken everything from this place before, and so Birdie drove on. The car crawled slowly through the road that took the Jeep right between the few buildings, this always made her feel uneasy, as though eyes were watching her, but she had to shake the feeling because she knew if they were watching her the growls and moans would be heard almost immediately, dead people didn't know how to be quiet anymore.

If it wasn't for the rumble of the engine, this place would have been dead quiet, the birds had died off long ago, unable to breathe the air here when the world had been at its most deadly, but that wasn't all, perhaps they had migrated away from humans, towards a place where there was nothing more than other wildlife roaming the earth. Surely the animals didn't rise from the grave?

When Birdie had first come here, she had taken to killing wildlife for food, sometimes the odd kangaroo had provided enough meat to keep some weight on her body, but now they were rare too, other humans had consumed the wildlife, gone back to the roots of humanity and started to live off the land again. The memory of coming across a dead boy with his head buried deep inside the gut of wallaby, teeth cracking and crunching through ribs and organs had confirmed that those dead things didn't just eat humans, but they consumed anything and everything in their path. Deep down they were still very much like the human race in some ways.

Birdie was forced to drive further out; she passed through two more deserted towns before she came across one she hadn't been to before. She pulled up to the side of the road just outside of the town and killed the engine and before she gathered her bag and weapons and headed into the ghost town by foot.

Birdie was on edge, and her eyes scanned the dust caked windows of the buildings before her, the silence was deafening, and she moved quietly, barely making a sound as she placed one foot in front of the other. She came to a convenience store and pushed open the door before her bright eyes peered into the shadows, scanning the room and then slipping inside. Birdie worked quickly, hand franticly grabbing things off the shelf, mostly items that were in cans or foil, things that wouldn't be full of rotten food inside. She gathered her things, slung the heavy pack over her back, as her shoulders began to sag with the weight, and gripped two litre bottles of water in each hand before she moved back outside, and towards the car. She shoved the items into the passenger seat, and started the engine, slowly rolling on into the town. She walked up to the petrol station and pumped fuel into the tank before Birdie slid the petrol pump back into place and opened the car door, as the familiar scraping and shuffling began.

48

She laid eyes on the creature as she checked over her shoulder. This was a child, barely four years old, with ringlets saturated in black, rotten blood, the fluids oozed over her forehead and into her right eye, before trailing down and onto her cheeks. The wound to her head was enormous; a gouge the size of a fist had been taken out of her skull, probably by the jaws of one of her own, and the contents of her brain was nothing more than black and brown sludge that slid like water down her skull. She wore a little pink dress, the hem fell to just above her knees. The fabric was stained in places with dirt and blood, and her limp was caused by the jagged femoral bone in her right thigh which protruded through decayed, black and cheese colored flesh.

Birdie stepped back, taking the gun and aimed it at the little girl's head, what was left of it anyway. Her heart beat drowned out the silence around her, and the snarling growls this dead child emitted weren't even something Birdie could hear anymore. Her finger rested on the trigger, and each step the dead child made closed the gap between them. Suddenly Birdie thrust the shot gun into the car, slid her arse onto the split leather seats and slammed the door, before locking it and slowly she drove towards the dead girl. As she passed it, the child twisted, chubby, black fingers scraped and grabbed at the driver's door. She pressed her grotesque, crumpled, grey face against the window, black and yellow ooze smearing onto the glass as Birdie thrust her foot onto the accelerator and sped away.

Birdie glanced into the rear vision mirror, the dust loomed up behind her like a cloud, but she could see a figure walking towards the girl, no he was running. It was a male figure, and he grabbed the little girl and began to pull her away. She slammed her foot hard on the brake pedal, skidding to a halt before Birdie turned and slowly drove back. Her eyes fell onto the man; he was tall, with long, black ragged hair. But he was too fast to be one of them, these creatures only ever dawdled. His clothes were worn and shredded and as she rolled down the window, his brilliant blue eyes locked onto hers.

"What the fuck are you doing?" she cried.

The man still gripped at the girl, his hands held her by the neck as she clawed at the air in front of her, those dead, glazed eyes saw nothing but a meal in the Jeep.

"Leave us alone" the man shouted, and he picked up the little dead girl, he carried her squirming body into a nearby abandoned house.

Birdie pulled up and jumped out of the car before following on their heels, the man turned to look at her, his eyes were wide with anger, "this has nothing to do with you." He yelled, trying to shut the old, wooden door behind him.

Birdie pushed at the door, using her body to force it open a crack, unable to let this go, "please let me in." She said, desperate to keep hold of the only human she had laid eyes on in over seven years.

The man sighed and finally opened the door; this allowed Birdie to walk in. He still had the child, and he placed shackles on her feet. She stood, chained to a rail on the wall, and she pulled continuously at the chains with thick drool dribbling over her snarling lips, her sunken eyes looked through the two of them.

The man stopped and stared at Birdie.

"What..." her voice trailed off, eyes unable to relinquish the stare she had locked onto that little child.

"She's my daughter." Said the man, and his face crumpled slightly, he sank down onto a steel chair, before he slowly looked up at the woman before him. Birdie shook her head in amazement, "She's a fucking..." her voice trailed off.

The man's eyes blazed with anger, "no, it's still Lilly somewhere in there."

"Why doesn't she bite you?" asked Birdie, as she shifted her weight from one foot to another nervously.

50

"Because..." the man swallowed, tears in his eyes, "because I pulled out her baby teeth, one by one with pliers," he leaned forward and offered his hand to the little girl, her gray mouth opened wide and her gums landed hungrily onto his flesh, suckling and attempting to chomp away like a starving animal, the wrinkled, grey flesh of her face pressed into his skin. He simply allowed it; the saliva trickled down his arm, as her heavy snorts filled the room.

Birdie couldn't believe this, she watched in disgust as the demonic little girl furiously tried to work at the flesh offered to her. "This...this is sick."

The man looked up, moving his arm away from the girl and wiping it on his shirt before replying, "She's all I have left in this world."

Birdie nodded slowly, unable to fully understand the situation. She had never conceived, so she didn't know what it was like to be a parent, but she could see the pain in the father's eyes. His black hair had the odd streak of silver, grey hairs intertwined with the rest of his wild mane. But he didn't look that old, perhaps in his late thirties.

She looked around the old, weatherboard house, before speaking again, this time in a lower voice, "And you've been here all this time?"

He shook his head, "No, not all this time. We came here a few weeks back. We're originally from Victoria, but once the disease spread, we came inland. The coast is thriving with...with..." his voice trailed off.

Birdie nodded, "When did she become one of them?"

"Three weeks ago," the man choked back tears, holding himself together.

"Look," Birdie said with compassion in her voice, "I have a place that's a lot safer than here. You could come with me."

The man looked up, "What about Lilly?"

She found herself glancing at the little child, still shuffling in the corner, "Are you certain her teeth can't grow back?"

The man nodded, "you've seen them, once they lose something it doesn't grow back. Not even baby teeth." He reached for a drawer, sliding out a pair of pliers, "but I have these just in case."

"Alright," Birdie said, "gather your things and let's go."

They chained the little girl to the back seat, binding her tight so that she couldn't get free though she struggled frantically, and then left that town. Heading back towards the sanctuary that Birdie had, when they pulled up, the sun had set, and the headlights illuminated the little cottage. There was nothing out here at the moment, so they easily opened the gates and went in. The man turned out to be called James, and he chained Lilly to the kitchen sink.

"Welcome to my humble home." Birdie said, and James sat down. They ate from cans that night, and as they did Birdie watched James open a third can, grabbing fists of cold spaghetti in his hands and feeding his demented daughter.

"You're wasting food." She murmured, and James looked up, wiggling white worms of spaghetti sliding through his fingers as he spoke, "she might die if we don't feed her."

"She's already dead." Birdie muttered.

As messed up as the situation was Birdie was grateful to have another human being in her life again, that gaping hole inside of her chest seemed to be less painful tonight. And as she curled up on the floor, with James nearby she tried to sleep. But the constant shuffling and moaning of the little girl was torturous to her mind. The fact that she had one of them inside of her home was terrifying.

Halfway through the night, Birdie found she had to give up on sleep altogether, and she decided to do a check of the perimeter. She walked silently past the dead girl, the gargling noises she made didn't seem to bother James, and he slept peacefully on the floor. But outside, Birdie noticed that when they'd been asleep something had tried to tear holes in the wire, she scrounged around for tin and boards to patch it up. Eventually happy with her work, but something about it was nerve racking. What was the point of keeping them out if they already had one in here?

She peered through the darkness, and it was quiet and still. The cool breeze gripped at what was left of her hair and whipped it around wildly. Eventually she settled back down on the floor of the shack, and lay there until morning.

"Good morning, Birdie" said James, leaning forward and tending to little Lilly as she spoke.

Birdie wiped her eyes, glancing up, "morning."

The little girl was snapping at her father with her gums, smacking her lips together as though he was nothing more than a platter ready to be served.

"How do you put up with that?" asked Birdie.

James didn't even look up as he spoke, "you get used to it."

Pulling back the blind, Birdie did her usual check outside; her eyes bulged with fear as she caught sight of the mob hanging around the perimeter.

"Holy fuck," she murmured.

James came over, frowning as he moved, peeking through the blind too. His body brushed against Birdie, causing her cheeks to flush slightly, "Where did they come from?"

"This hasn't happened before, not this many, there must be twenty of them out there." Birdie exclaimed. She turned to look at James, "do they follow you?"

James shook his head, "we've bumped into a few, but Lilly and I are usually on the move." He paused, glancing back at his daughter, her moans were growing louder now, and the mob outside were still pressing at the wire, pushing on it at random places.

"You fucking liar," Birdie cried, stepping back from the window and staring at James with wild eyes, "they follow her don't they!" she shouted, pointing at the chained creature in the kitchen.

Lilly was throwing her weight against the chains now, and the old sink was creaking in agony.

James looked at her, tears welled in his eyes "I'm sorry Birdie. You know I can't give her back to them."

"What do you mean?" she cried, her palms shoved into James' chest hard, pushing him back suddenly "You took her?"

With a shocked face, James stumbled backward, before speaking, "I did."

Birdie whirled around, staring at the girl, "is she even your daughter?"

"Biologically, no" James moved forward, blocking Birdie's path, stopping her from moving towards Lilly, "I found her like this, and I couldn't leave her."

"You idiot" Screamed Birdie, grabbing at the zombie child frantically, "You have to give her back."

James gripped at Birdie's wrists, holding her still with his hands, "Never, I love her like my own child."

The mass of bodies were pushing up against the wire outside now, working as one, their weight began to force the wire to bend and the steel to warp, the noise was deafening as the constant growling, snorts and groans filled Birdie's world.

She slumped in James' arms, looking up at him helplessly, "I know you've been alone. I have too. I realize you took her because you wanted someone, anything is better than being alone." Her words were rushed, voice urgent, "but James, she's one of them and they will stop at nothing to get to her, to get to us.

54

I don't know how they followed her, but she has led them straight to you, straight to me."

James stared at Birdie, eyes welling with tears as they began to roll down his face.

"Please James, let her go. Stay with me." Birdie cried out over the noise around her.

James glanced over his shoulder, Lilly was distressed, throwing her weight furiously against the chains, the kitchen sink was still groaning as she did so, suddenly her left ankle snapped, collapsing slightly as the tibia and fibula bones tore through the dead, grey skin.

"Quickly, we have to get out now, while we're still alive." Birdie yelled.

The kitchen sink came off the wall, and the child began to drag herself closer to James, stumbling on her broken ankles, her dead hands grabbed at his clothing, tearing strips off the shirt. She sunk her toothless mouth into his hip, chewing feverishly; James placed a single hand on the little girls' neck.

"I love you, Lilly." He said, before yanking himself free from the child's grip and taking Birdies hand. They dashed to the door and grabbed the bag of goods, revolver and shotgun as they went, jumping into the car and turning it on. Birdie backed out, and pulled the car face to face with the gate, the mob was thick with dead, rotting flesh and grotesque bodies, snarling faces ready to greet them.

Birdie turned to James, handing him the shot gun, a revolver in her hand, "Shoot." She said, as her foot hit the accelerator.

The Jeep burst forward, bulbar colliding with the gate, chains snapping and the fence exploded open, sending bodies flying in every direction, Birdie drove with her foot flat to the ground, bullets launching into the air before her and exploding into the faces and skull of the creatures. The car crashed into some, their faces hitting the windshield and causing the glass to crack, black, brown and red flesh smeared and streaked its way over the windscreen. James shot too, blowing giant holes into the skulls of some, and the guts of others. Hands gripped at the doors, open mouths pressed to the windows and revealed thick black tongues and jagged teeth.

James and Birdie left the sanctuary behind in a cloud of dust. And as they drove, Birdie reached out and placed her hand into his, whispering, "We'll be okay."

* * * *

They made their way along the road, leaving the place Birdie once called home. Finally they came to a stop at a small, deserted town. Exhausted, Birdie set a blanket on the ground, curling up and sleeping.

When Birdie woke up, she found herself bound at the wrists and ankles, terrified she tried to sit up, struggling against the restraints, but was unable to, her wide eyes locked onto the face before her, James sat nearby smiling.

"What are you doing?" Birdie cried, terror gripping at her heart.

"Making you mine." He said and leaned over, a large rock clenched in his hand, before raising it and slamming it into Birdie's skull.

And everything went black.

The next time Birdie came around, the agony in her head and mouth was insane, she gargled and spluttered, spitting out thick wads of metallic blood, as James moved her head, allowing her vomit the gunk out of her mouth. She tried to speak, but the pain was too much, and her voice slurred, body shaking.

James sat back, watching the bound woman, blood leaked from her mouth and trailed down her chin in black and red puddles, coagulating in thick clumps on the ground. He wiped the blood off his own hands, setting the pliers on the table beside the pile teeth he had extracted from her gums, some had been pulled clean out, tiny roots curling up from the tooth itself, others were broken and chipped. James picked her up, Birdie sagged in his arms like a dead weight, tears sliding down her face and saturating his arms, he placed her in the back of the car and drove back to the sanctuary.

Once there, he grabbed her struggling body, Birdie wriggled and squirmed but the blood loss had taken its toll on her body, and then he dumped her nearby, sitting in the car and watching as what was left of the mob began to move towards Birdie, her screams echoed through the night as they sunk jagged, rotten teeth into her flesh, crouching over her and pressing their demonic faces into the caverns they were creating, lifting their heads every once in a while to reveal wrinkled faces smeared with blood and hungry mouths chewing strips of red, raw meat. He got out of the car, closing the door gently, and walking over, before placing a bullet into the two dead guys eating his friend. She whimpered on the ground, a large chunk of flesh had been devoured from her belly, leaving a gaping hole in her abdomen. Glistening, wet, sausage like intestines leaked from the wound, perforated in places, and her own feces leaked out and onto the dirt. James simply watched on as her skin began to turn a sickly pale grey, and Birdie slipped into a coma.

James collected the shackles from the sanctuary, and attached them to the dead woman's ankles, before placing her into the car and driving off.

This was his new Lilly. And he knew once she had transformed she would be with him forever.

I Walk, Therefore I Am
by Ryan Neil Falcone

I snap awake, appalled to discover that my mouth is filled with dirt. I gag trying to spit it out, but when I try to reach to clear it away, my hand remains locked in place, motionless. The world around me is dark, silent, and numbingly cold. I can't remember how I got here. My head is pounding so badly that I can barely think.

Panicked, I begin to thrash. At first nothing happens, but slowly the dirt around me gives way. As more of it loosens, the soil around me churns as I claw my way toward the surface.

I recoil when my digging hands brush against a severed leg. As I continue to dig, I come across other corpses that have been similarly interred. The earth I'm buried in reeks of their putrescence, and if my mouth weren't already clogged with dirt, I'd scream.

I'm desperate to get out of this mass grave, but my frantic movements work against me and all I seem to be doing is digging myself deeper. Just when the claustrophobia closes in on me, my hand breaks through. Encouraged, I fumble around the ground above me, seeking any handhold I can use to pull myself up. After a few minutes, I manage to wiggle my head above the surface. I spit the dirt from my mouth with disgust, and take a deep breath—thankful to be free from the accursed soil.

After I've pulled my entire body free, I crawl away from the sinking maw, exhausted. I only make it a few feet before I spot another set of wiggling fingers stabbing skyward from the dirt. Someone else is buried down there! I slither forward through the mud, oblivious to the risk of sliding back into the fissure I've just escaped. I need to help whoever is trapped underground.

I reach forward to clasp the protruding hand, and I'm surprised when it clamps down on mine with the strength of a vice. I reposition my body and dig my heels into the soil, hoping to use my leverage to help free whoever is buried down there. But as the person I'm helping begins to emerge, the flesh disappears a few inches down from the hand I'm holding and the arm turns skeletal, and when the buried person's head comes into view, I'm face-to-face with a decomposing corpse. One eye is missing—most of that side of its face is missing. The one staring at me is putrefied—like the eye of a dead fish. But what's even more horrible is the unmistakable ember of sentience burning behind the film covering the rotting eye.

I throw myself backwards, but the creature won't let go. I keep pulling until I both hear and feel a sickening tear when its arm rips free from its shoulder. My legs piston as I scramble backwards away from the hole. Its severed arm still clings to me, but I wedge the stump between my feet and manage to wrench my hand loose.

I clamber awkwardly to my feet, desperate to get away from this madness, but it doesn't take long for my uncooperative limbs to tangle, sending me crashing to the ground before I've stumbled even a few yards. From this vantage point, on my hands and knees, I finally take stock of the surreal, unnatural scene unfolding around me.

I'm in the athletic fields behind the high school. Dozens of earthen mounds are scattered throughout what used to be the baseball field. The dead are everywhere, digging themselves free from these mounds. An explosion in the distance makes me jump. Fires burn somewhere nearby, a plume of ominous black smoke mars the evening sky. I recognize the sound of the town's tornado siren buzzing above the din of the ghoulish activity around me like a persistent swarm of hornets.

My jaw drops, and I'm barely aware that I can still taste dirt on my tongue. My relentless headache makes it difficult to make sense out of what's happening around me. I can't even remember my name.

Dozens of jumbled images flash through my mind, but my blinding migraine makes it difficult to make sense of the garbled memories. I wince at a particularly acute flash of pain, but closing my eyes helps me to momentarily shut out the distractions around me and organize my thoughts.

My hometown…Syracuse, Kansas…population 1,800…the train derailing just outside of town…the chemical spill…the military quarantine…the poisonous green vapor cloud settling in the town cemetery…

I shake my head to clear away these disjointed images—but I can't. I remember the dead bursting from their graves and descending upon the town like a plague of insatiable locusts. I can picture the hastily-constructed military blockade that prevented the townsfolk from leaving, and the army's abandonment of the town after their efforts to contain the situation failed. Then, the sheriff's department organized a group of local volunteers to help protect the town from the shambling monstrosities.

None of which explains who I am or how I came to be buried a mass grave behind the high school.

My hand dips to my pocket, tracing against my wallet. I pull it out and try to coax my fumbling, unresponsive fingers to unfold the brown leather. Before I succeed, I'm suddenly aware that I'm not alone. Two of the walking dead are moving toward me. They lurch forward—gnashing their teeth in anticipation while maggot's squirm in the open wounds on their bodies—and as I cower before them, they unexpectedly veer off and move away as if disinterested. The question of why they've left me alone no sooner forms in my mind before the explanation occurs to me.

My headache returns with renewed vigor, but I grit my teeth and try to suppress the crippling pain that makes it so difficult to think. I steadfastly refuse to accept the conclusion I'd reached moments before. If I were dead, why would I feel pain from my headache? And doesn't being able to think prove that I'm alive?

Despite these rationalizations, I think about the buried zombie I'd unwittingly tried to help, and I'm reminded of the glimmer of intelligence burning in its eye. That's when the world starts to spin. I close my eyes.

None of this makes any sense—the creatures that attacked the town showed no signs of intelligence…they'd been monsters, driven to attack and consume the living. I'm nothing like them. There has to be some mistake—maybe I was buried accidentally. This thought is interrupted by a frightening, new series of images.

A group of us making an armed stand in the town hall, fighting a losing battle to fend off the endless horde of walking dead… the door shatters, and the dead stream into the lobby when the barricade fails… being cornered by a group of walking dead while I frantically tried to reload my rifle…

A lump forms in my throat, and when I choke it down, I can still taste dirt when I swallow. My hands descend, tracing over the disemboweled midsection concealed by my blood-stained shirt—and all at once a cold stillness fills my mind.

My trembling hands still hold my wallet. I crack it open and stare at the driver's license, reading and re-reading the information.

Jonathan Mills.
54 Sycamore Lane.
Syracuse, Kansas.

I stare at my picture, and it doesn't take long for a deluge of memories to come flooding back. I can't believe I couldn't remember before. I've lived in this town my whole life. My father died when I was fourteen-years-old. I played baseball in high school. I sell insurance. My wife's name is Sarah. We met in college. We have three children—Jonathan, Jr., Naomi, and Jamie...

I'm suddenly gripped by a sense of sorrow so powerful it's staggering. As much as I want to shut the memory out, I'm powerless to prevent myself from seeing...

...Jamie, our youngest, attacked by a group of walking dead in our front yard the day of the chemical spill... shouting as I race from our front porch to help her, followed by Jonathon, Jr....the echo of my wife's screams as I run toward the mangled body of our six-year old daughter, who's being eviscerated on our front lawn...

I double over, one hand clutching my mangled midsection, the other on my forehead. When I howl in anguish, nobody pays attention. The walking dead, it seems, have their own agenda.

Panic suddenly overwhelms me again. My family—are they safe? I drop my wallet and stagger away from the high school, toward town. The fires burning in the distance keep that side of night in twilight—and I head in that direction like a moth drawn to the flame, toward home.

I lurch along the road's right shoulder, frustrated by my inability to move faster. All around me swarms a procession of walking dead. I can feel my headache returning, but I try to fight it off by focusing upon elusive memories of my family. The nightmarish landscape around me disappears, replaced by a vision from earlier that summer: one of my son's little league games.

Sitting next to me on the bleachers, Sarah inserts two fingers into her mouth and whistles, cheering on our son who is up to bat. Next to her, I jump to my feet and begin to cheer when he swings the aluminum bat he's holding and cracks a line drive into the outfield...

This joyous memory is replaced by a more disturbing one—of me bludgeoning Jonathan, Jr. relentlessly with the very same aluminum bat after he'd been bitten by his youngest sister, who'd transformed into a monster moments after she'd died on the front lawn.

The sustained blast of an automobile horn behind me dissipates this wretched memory. Surprised, I glance over my shoulder and I'm blinded by the headlights of a car bearing down on me. I freeze when it swerves toward me, knowing that I won't be able to move out of the way fast enough. At the very last second, the car changes direction and plows into a pair of walking dead to my left. They explode in a shower of decomposing flesh and curdled bodily fluids, and the car passes so close to me that I make eye contact with the teenagers inside. I expect them to turn around, but the car doesn't even slow down—its red taillights growing dimmer as they drive off down the road.

Shaken, I move further onto the shoulder to make myself as inconspicuous as possible. I can't let anything stop me from getting to my family.

When my headache returns in full force, I embrace it— grateful to banish these hurtful memories from conscious thought. My instincts guide me through the streets of our neighborhood. Although I can't remember what my house looks like, the address from my license burns in my memory. 54 Sycamore Lane.

My mind rises from behind the curtain of oblivion I've willingly draped over it when I arrive at our street. Immediately, I recognize that something is amiss: the entire street is dark and eerily silent, as if it's been abandoned. The only discernible noise emanates from town, where the blare of the tornado siren still shrieks. Something must be happening in town for the siren to be going off, but I can't remember what it is. My headache prevents me from remembering what I'm doing here.

It's not until I'm standing in front of my house that I remember. With renewed purpose, I lurch toward my house, eager to see my family again.

Dark sheets cover the front windows, but I detect a faint flicker of light emanating from a window near the back of the house. I stagger toward the back door, pressing my face against the window to peer inside.

Sarah and Naomi are sitting on the floor in the middle of the living room. My wife's face, illuminated by flickering candle light, is gaunt. I watch her nervously stroke our sleeping daughter's hair, feeling an overwhelming sense of relief to see that they are safe.

When I try to knock on the back door to get their attention, my uncooperative hand inadvertently breaks through the window pane. Sarah's scream from inside the house induces me to push open the barricaded door and rush inside to reassure them that they needn't be frightened.

I'm confused by the naked terror in their eyes…puzzled by their fear when they recognize who I am. I try to explain that I'm still alive, but my throat feels like it's filled with gravel. The only noise I'm able to make is a mindless groan.

I knock over a table as I stagger toward them…angered by my inability to communicate. Their screams are maddening and trigger the return of my headache, this time with renewed intensity. If they'd just be quiet and listen…

I'll make them listen.

When the red haze clears—after I'm done engorging myself upon my family—I stare at the carnage in disbelief, unable to accept what I've done. I stare at my hands, covered with their blood, and feel my mind snap. I tear the living room apart, but even this rampaging destruction doesn't mask the evidence of the atrocity I've committed.

Overcome by guilt, I flee the house and stagger toward town, determined to end this wretched mockery of life. I deserve to die for what I've done. That's the only thing that makes sense to me anymore.

As I approach town, I join a legion of the walking dead—drawn to the commotion in the town. I wonder if they're like me—whether they can think. Does it even matter? My only focus is finding a way to get myself killed.

I can't remember why anymore.

As we approach the town square, my attention is drawn by the sound of gunfire. Nearby, a group of townsfolk shoot at us from behind a pile of stacked debris. I stumble toward them, trying to separate myself from the larger group. I'm frustrated when several others follow me, lurching alongside me toward these survivors.

Several members of the advancing horde around me are gunned down. I try to wave my arms to get the shooters' attention, but I'm only able to raise my arms in front of me to shoulder height. It seems impossible that none of the bullets whizzing past my head find the mark as I approach the barricade.

I climb over the blockade, moving toward the nearest gunman…determined to give him one final opportunity to put a bullet in my brain. But when he levels his rifle at my head and pulls the trigger, nothing happens. His gun is empty. The unfortunate man screams when I knock it from his hands and descend upon him—suddenly ravenous.

I mindlessly tear the man's throat open and begin to feed. The sound of his rifle bouncing on the pavement is muffled when it comes to rest in a pool of crimson spreading outward below us as the red haze descends upon me once again.

And the Weeds Shook with Laughter
by John M. Edwards

Luther Pendragon took hold of the body and began dragging it out of the mausoleum across the recently mown grass, smelling like female arousal. He looked around to make sure absolutely no one else was around and plopped down to consult his ancient book of magic spells--which he had found on Amazon.com by sheer happenstance.

The wind picked up a little, and the cicadas created a stirring reluctant symphony, which oddly enough sounded a little like it was part of Wagner's "Ring Cycle." Luther liked Classical music, and so did his friends: "Axel Rose."

The silence radiated like a nicotine buzz.

"Let's see," he flipped through the fragile parchment pages and landed on the right god named "THULE."

"Looother!" came a too-loud voice.

"Yo, Looother!" came another trebled up a notch.

"We're watching you!" came yet another *volte face.*

And the weeds shook with laughter.

Great, Luther's old high-school chums insisted on taking the mickey out of him. None of them were college material.

Luther, on the other hand, was a proud graduate of Union County College, even though he had resigned himself long ago to taking over the family business, or plot.

And the weeds shook with laughter.

They could at least have helped him deliver the corpse, "John B. Stone (1990-2020)," over to the campfire, one of the greatest athletes to ever appear in their forlorn town, and the only student that didn't make fun of him.

His heart had exploded on the playing field.

And the weeds shook with laughter.

"Loother!"

"Loother!

"Loother!"

A rather menacing gust of atmosphere passed over the cemetery, blowing Luther's Yankees cap off, even though the gibbous moon eyed the pathetic pastoral landscape like a muscle-bound bouncer burning with revenge.

And the weeds shook with laughter.

He couldn't believe that Nora actually liked him after all these years, since they had barely said a word to each other in high school, yet there she was standing in an ethereal Medieval-like gown ready to give "Dungeons & Dragons" a try.

"Luther, can I help you?"

"Well yeah, tell Dave, Bob, and Mark to keep their mouths shut. We could get in trouble if we're caught."

"But you are the attendant of this graveyard. Nobody will ever know." He was sure the weird look on her face was an instinctive repulsion to his red hair and freckles. He was glad she was here though, in fact very relieved. He hadn't seen her in years; in fact he hadn't seen her since she had wanly walked the fluorescent corridors of his *alma mater* dating all of his friends except for him.

And the weeds shook with laughter.

Luther was crackerjack at starting campfires, and he hence muttered the spell sounding like Gaelic, but which was really a dialect from the Rhineland. The only real friends Luther had ever had were "green" and "orange." Even so, they had menaced him for years with their UPS jobs by delivering Yuletide gifts of inedible "fruit cakes."

Revenge was never an option in this small New Jersey town where everyone knew everybody else's business.

And the weeds shook with laughter.

Luther chucked the corpse on the campfire with a mean look on his face, as Dave wearing a bandana came over and slapped him hard on the back.

Bob and Mark, looking hung-over and worse for wear, then slowly approached the crackling glow of the campfire. However, Nora watched the proceedings at a distance like a self-satisfied cat with canny eyes who was either unwilling or unable to put out.

He watched as his fair-weather friends, whom he had brought back, devoured their high-school hero. However, Luther confined himself to eating an Oscar-Meyer all-beef frank on a stick, plus a few marshmallows.

They ate and drank and laughed far into the night.

The Meat Lover's Special
by Miracle Austin

For 60 seconds, Dash contemplated driving away from her
life and never looking back. Instead, she threw her sweater onto
the driver's leather seat and slid down.

The steering wheel burnt her fingers upon touch. She
jerked them back.

She popped in the car key, turned over the ignition, and
pressed the air conditioner button to full blast.

The tortuous Texas heat barely allowed for cool air to
tickle her face.

She scooted in her seat, peeling her dress from the back of
her sweaty thighs, which felt like sticky flypaper. Her phone
chirped.

Dash reached behind her backseat to hunt for it in her
stuffed purse. Her pursed tumbled onto the floor, spilling all
contents—cosmetics and a **.38 Special**.

She found it after the third ring and placed it on speaker.

"Hey, babe, I'm on my way home. I'll start the steaks, as
soon as I jump in the shower," Jeremy, her fiancée, said.

"What?"

"Don't tell me you forgot that Vince and Stacie were coming over tonight?"

"Yeah, I guess I did," as she reached back with her right hand to throw all the contents back into her purse. "Be home as soon as I can."

The call ended.

Dash shifted the car in reverse, sped out of the driveway, and drove toward the market to retrieve two T-bone steaks, bag of salad, baked potatoes, red wine, cheese cubes, crackers, pound cake, fresh strawberries, and glaze.

When she arrived at home, she saw Vince and Stacie walking towards the front door.

Dash pushed the yellow garage door button on a panel above her and drove in.

She hopped out of the car, throwing her purse over her shoulder, while scooping the paper grocery bags into her arms, and leaped towards the back door.

Without paying any attention to the one bag with the red wine, it gave away. The bottle dropped and splattered onto the kitchen floor, as soon as she opened the door.

Jeremy heard the noise from the living room, where he was entertaining Vince and Stacie.

"Hey, you guys, I'll be back. I think Dash needs some help."

"Sure, we'll surf through *BlueFlix*," Vince replied, grabbing the television remote from the coffee table.

Dash was kneeled down on the floor picking up the large broken, glass pieces from the floor and wiping the red wine up with towels she pulled from the shelf next to her off the floor, as fast as she could.

"Jeremy, I'm so sorry about the wine. I'll run back to the market to pick up another bottle."

"Never mind. Stacie brought over a bottle. Why do you always mess things up?" he whispered, pinching Dash hard under her right arm.

"Ouch, Jeremy, you're hurting me. Let go." She jerked her arm back from him, while staring down at her purse on the floor.

He shrugged his shoulders, "If you would just do what I ask, then things would be perfect. I told you to pick up the groceries earlier this week."

"Honey, I'm sorry. What else you want me to say?"

"Toss me those damn steaks, so I can put them on the grill for Vince and me. Wait until later. Don't think I'll forget about this little stunt."

Dash rushed to the bedroom, peeled out of the sweaty work clothes, jumped in shower for a quick wash-off, dried herself, and threw on a backless white summer dress. She then slipped on white tennis shoes.

She dropped two drops of <u>Visine</u> in both eyes, popped an Ativan in her mouth, and took a few deep breaths.

She walked back into the kitchen to prepare the salad, cheese-crackers, and dessert.

"Hey Stacie and Vince," she said.

Stacie and Vince walked up to the island and hugged her.

"So good to see you guys. It's been awhile. You look great," Stacie shared.

"Thanks. We've been so busy with work and wedding planning," Dash said.

"Hey, Vince, grab us some beers from the fridge," Jeremy yelled out, as he poked his narrow head through the sliding door to scan the room like a military laser before exterminating its target.

"Dash, I thought you were going to wear the brown outfit."

"Oh, it makes me look fat, Jeremy. I thought this one looked better. See," she half twirled.

"Vince and Stacie, come on out and enjoy some music and beer outside. The wine is in the cooler," he said.

"Sure, come on Stacie," Vince said, grabbing the beers from the fridge and placing under his arms, as he shoved Stacie out with his body. They walked outside and sat down in the cushioned chairs.

Jeremy stormed back in and shut the door behind him softly.

Dash's hands began to quiver like being submerged into freezing water.

Jeremy turned six shades of red within seconds.

"Why are you always challenging me?"

"I wasn't Jeremy. I just thought this would be a better choice for the occasion."

His hands rested on his hips. The back of his right hand swung towards her mouth faster than any baseball pitcher's fastball.

Blood droplets exploded from her mouth and flung onto the front of the fridge. She fell down to the floor, pulling the salad on top of her.

He stooped down next to her.

"Now, you have to change. Put on what I told you. Hurry up. Our friends are waiting for dinner. Clean this mess up and you too." He scooped up the baked potatoes.

She grabbed a dishtowel, held it to her mouth, pressed down gently, and shuffled to the bathroom to change into the khaki baggy pantsuit.

Dash stared up in the mirror, unzipping her stained dress. Thick tracks were painted under her eyes, left from her running black eyeliner. She wiped her running nose with the back of hand towel resting on top of the wood counter.

The water faucets were turned on slowly to rinse her face. She then sat down in her vanity chair and opened up a drawer, where over a dozen hospital, emergency room ID plastic bracelets covered up her makeup.

She shoved them to one side, picked up the tube of concealer makeup, and squeezed a quarter-size onto her fingertips and blended it around her mouth area. The concealer powder came next with a few dabs of neutral gloss onto her lips.

Dash re-entered the kitchen, swept up the salad off the kitchen floor, and wiped the blood off the fridge's door with paper towels dipped in warm soapy water.

She opened up the fridge and rummaged through. Luckily, she found a half head of lettuce, two plump tomatoes, and a few carrot sticks in the back of a drawer.

A second salad was prepared.

She walked out onto the patio with a tray where the salad bowl, dressings, and cheese-crackers rested.

"Okay, you guys let's begin," she said.

"Hey, why did you change, Dash? Your dress was so lovely," Stacie said.

"I spilled something on it." She stared down at the grass.

"You okay, Dash?" Stacie asked.

"Yeah, just a tough week. Here have some salad."

They all sat down to eat, while Dash served the salad.

"Jeremy, my man, you know how I love my steak. Just enough grilling to knock that chill off. I love mine warm and bloody. I just don't get it how our girls are vegans," Vince said with a stuffed mouth.

"Yeah, me too, man. There's nothing like a juicy steak and a cold one." A few drops of blood ran down the side of Jeremy's mouth and down his hairy arms.

Stacie looked at Dash from across the table, as she nibbled some on her salad and baked potato, mostly scooting the food around her plate with her fork.

After dinner, they all went back into the house to watch a movie and to have dessert and wine.

Dash cleaned up, as she listened to her favorite jazz station.

Stacie walked into the kitchen to help her.

"Stacie, I got this. Please enjoy the movie."

"It's too loud and the movie switched to football. You know how it goes. Is there something wrong, Dash?"

"Nothing. Why do you ask?" She scrubbed the plate with the dishtowel repeatedly without looking up at her.

"It's written all over your face, Dash."

"I'm just tired."

"Okay, if you say so. I'm just going to keep bugging you, until you tell me."

Suddenly, a breaking news report interrupted the station.

"Emergency, emergency…if you have purchased any beef products from J's Grocery, Emma's Market, or K&M Whole Foods, then please throw out immediately! All meats contaminated. Repeat throw out. Please call 1-800-000-0000 for more information."

"Oh, my gosh, Dash. Where did those steaks come from?" Stacie asked as her knees began to wobble. She slid down into the barstool.

Dash slowly walked over to the trashcan. She lifted up some plastic bags with tossed salad on top and found the white paper, where the steaks had been wrapped in. She turned it over. It read: "*Emma's Market.*"

She dropped it to the floor.

Stacie ran over to her.

"Give me the phone, Stacie." Dash commanded without blinking.

Dash dialed the number. A rep answered.

"Hello, I just heard the news report on the radio about the contaminated beef. My fiancée and his friend just consumed steaks super-rare from *Emma's Market*."

78

"Listen, you need to get out of the house now!" the rep yelled.

"What? Why? What is it contaminated with?" Dash asked frantically.

"That's not important. Get out now! You may have less than 15 minutes with consumption before…" the rep replied, breathing hard and stuttering into the receiver.

"Please, tell me. What is it contaminated with?…Before what?"

"Mam, ticks were genetically engineered with a lethal flesh-eating virus in a lab a few months ago, about 60 miles from your location. Somehow they escaped and fed on a pasture of cattle. Those same cattle were unknowingly slaughtered and packaged into those stores listed from the announcement."

"So, you're telling me that my fiancé and our friend are going to eat me like in those silly zombie movies?"

"Yes, that's exactly what I'm trying to tell you. Listen, whoever consumed the contaminated meat will transform into a mad-human and feeding zombie with no memory of anything or anyone. I got your location and a special termination squad will be headed to your home address soon."

"I can't believe this."

"Believe it, sister. You really need to leave. Get out of there while you still can!," the rep demanded.

The phone call dropped with an irritating, dreadful buzz.

Dash repeated everything to Stacie.

"Stacie, we need to go now!"

"I'm not leaving, Vince. Someone's playing an awful joke, that's all Dash. None of it is true. It's just a big fat hoax to scare us on the radio. Remember, that radio segment years ago by that famous guy that caused panic to so many listeners? This is the same thing," Stacie whined.

"Come with me, Stacie. I really think the rep is telling the truth. Anyhow, I almost didn't come home today. I was going to leave Jeremy for good. I know this is my out."

"What?"

"Stacie, I didn't want to tell you, but he's been battering me for months."

"Dash, are you sure?"

"Yes, I think I would know."

"He doesn't mean to hurt you. Vince has hit me too, but not lately because I know what irritates him now. Men get angry and this is how they react. It's normal. You just have to figure out the things you do to cause Jeremy's irritation and stop doing those things. He's always telling Vince how the two of you are meant to be together."

"Are you kidding me? You think what Vince has done to you is forgivable? I should listen?"

"Of course…Vince is a good man. He works hard, so does Jeremy. Give him another chance. They don't mean it. It hurts them just as much, Dash."

"No, I can't believe this. Tonight was it for me! Come with me Stacie please, before something really bad happens."

"I can't."

Stacie hugged her.

Dash grabbed her purse off the counter and pulled out the **.38 Special**.

"Here, take this, at least." Dash attempted to hand it over to her.

Stacie pushed it away, hugged Dash, and walked back into the living room.

"Hey you guys? What are you two doing?" Stacie asked nervously.

Vince and Jeremy were hunched over on all fours behind the couch, as their bodies flinched again and again.

80

Stacie walked over to them with her arms pressed against her sides, touching her mini-ruffled skirt. Her legs shook like jello. Within seconds, their heads cocked backwards like a gun trigger. Thick yellow drool ran from their mouths. Their eyes widened and transformed into bright iridescent lenses. Their incisors protruded out and fixed themselves on her voluptuous thighs.

Dash was already in the car, backing out of the garage, and driving toward a black van parked in front of the house.

She heard Stacie scream twice and saw quick shadows move across the living room bay window.

Bold white initials, were printed on the side of the van, which read: **Z.T.** with **Zombie Terminators** spelled out underneath. The driver pointed a luminous, green light at Dash's eyes and waved her on.

She drove past her house for the last time.

The Zombie Appeal
by D. E. Cowen

FROM THE CASE FILES OF WALTER WALKER JOHNSON, ESQ.
PRIVILIEGED ATTORNEY WORK PRODUCT

Memorandum to: The File

From: *WWJ*

Re: Doe v. Victim-Closed File Memorandum

This is a concluded matter as a result of the 4-4 tie ruling by the U.S. Supreme Court upholding the ruling of the Coastal Circuit Court of Appeals regarding the permanent injunction against the stalking and eradication of so-called "infected humans" due to the application of the equal protection clause of the 14th Amendment as applied to the states.

Paid In full....closed "Firm Special"

NEWSWIRE
National Press
Galveston, Texas

The University of Galveston Medical Branch at Galveston announced the receipt of a grant from the Cook Foundation and the U.S. Department of Defense for the construction of its Infectious Research Center. Allaying the concerns of locals fearing the accidental release of one or more of the numerous deadly viruses that will be housed at the IRC, UGMB officials told National Press that security at the facility will be the best in the world. Also, the building will be pressured negatively to prevent any viruses or toxins studied at the facility from escaping. If a release is detected by the hundreds of monitors that will be installed at the IRC, the building will automatically lock down and air ventilation will be re-circulated to prevent release to the outside. "Even if something did get out," Professor Ira Dedin, chief virologist at the Center stated, "it would be so diluted by the time it actually reached the outside air that no one could possibly be affected. With Galveston being a upper coast barrier island, the sea breezes would immediately blow anything out to sea" Members of the community including Jennifer Watson, a member of the island's Historical Preservation and Volunteer Society organized protests at the ground breaking calling the IRC's position "a foolish exercise in hubris jeopardizing the entire fate of the community and beyond." Another person who asked not to be named questioned the role of the military in the facility. Galveston is a barrier island on the Texas Gulf Coast approximately 55 miles from downtown Houston. The mayor of Galveston, Ed Wopner welcomed the many jobs he said the new facility would bring to the island. "It's a glorious dawn of a new day for the Island," he said.

NEWSWIRE
National Press
Galveston, Texas

Exactly one year after its groundbreaking the University of Galveston Medical Branch at Galveston officially opened its doors and began research. 'This is a great day for science and humanity," said Professor Ira Dedin, chief virologist at the Center. Immediately upon its opening, reports surfaced of a number of large green trucks with U.S. Department of Defense insignias pulling up to the back of the facility. Reporters were not allowed to get near the openings and the IRC spokesperson would not comment on this activity. Ms. Jennifer Watson, president of the island's Historical Preservation and Volunteer Society issued a press release stating that, "Galveston Island has had the privilege of preserving its way of life for many years. The opening of this facility and the reports of these obviously military related shipments to the facility threatens everything we stand for."

NEWSWIRE
National Press
Galveston, Texas

Officials at the University of Galveston Medical Branch at Galveston's Infectious Research Center have issued the following press release:

The University acknowledges that due to faulty construction of the IRC which opened its doors just three months ago, the ventilation system of the IRC was reversed allowing air from sealed laboratories to be released directly into the HVAC system's common air vents and plenum. However, the situation has been corrected and there was no threat to employees or the community at large. An internal investigation into the failure of the security system to warn the center has been initiated.

The University also acknowledges that Dr. Ira Dedin, chief virologist at the IRC has not reported to work for several days. The University does not believe that Dr. Dedin's apparent disappearance is in any way related to the HVAC system issue. At the request of Dr. Dedin's family, anyone who may have knowledge of his whereabouts is requested to please notify the local police.

Client Interviews and Notes

Memorandum to: **WWJ**
From: Nancy Bailey
Re: Client Interview- Jennifer Watson- Walk-in

Walt. Please, please come down here and speak to this woman who just walked in. She's a nutter. And, I think she's carrying a large pistol in a paper bag. She doesn't look like one of the freaks that have been getting around in the area. I don't like bothering you but you are the only partner who doesn't play golf on Fridays. Nance.

Memorandum To: The Partners of the Firn
From: **WWJ**
Re: Doe v. Victim- Client Interview- Jennifer Watson

Jennifer Watson presented herself today as a potential new client. She is in her mid-40s, attractive with dyed blonde hair, poofed up with dark streak which may be deemed by juries to be severe. She seemed extremely upset. The receptionist sent an email memo to me to deal with her thinking that she may be armed and may have been another recently escaped patient from James Bealey Psych Hospital at UGMB.

I have met her previously at local historical preservation fund raisers. Ms. Watson verified that she did indeed possess a .457 magnum in a paper bag. She assured me that she was not crazy or a "freak." Instead, she said that she was being sued because she had been attacked at her home by persons she called "mutant zombie freaks" two weeks before.

I recall an article in the back of the paper back then, but that was around the time all these outbreaks of hospital ward crazies going around town started.

Jennie said that on that particular night these persons broke through the kitchen door of her house and grabbed two of her children before she knew what was happening. Hearing them scream, she and her husband Neil ran into the kitchen with a baseball bat from the den and found the freaks eating, yes eating, her children. They had already ripped out the soft areas of their bodies when Neil attempted to hit them with the bat. Before he could raise his bat again they had pinned Neil to the floor and were ripping off his flesh as he screamed. I expressed my condolences. She thanked me and said that the experienced had numbed her from emotional pain.

Ms. Watson explained to me that she retrieved her husband's shotgun from a closet and loaded it. She went into the kitchen shaking with fear and fired. The first shot struck one of the "mutant zombie freaks" as she called them in the head. She said that the thing's head erupted as if full of a noxious gas and the attacker dropped dead. She said she fired at another freak but only struck it in the stomach. This apparently had no effect and did not deter the thing from chewing on her husband's ears. She shot once more, again striking the head with the same effect as the other. It was then she said she realized that only shooting them in the head would have any effect.

After shooting four more, the attackers left. She tried to call the police but discovered that the police reported that hers was one of several incidents that night. She went to a neighbor's house to find that her neighbor had been attacked as well. She organized a group of her neighbors collecting guns and ammunition. Together they found a police car and convinced the policeman driving the vehicle to assist them in hunting down more of these so-called freaks.

She explained that over the course of the past week, her "zombie hunter" gang, as she called them, became one of several such groups hunting and killing these things. I recall that the police have issued warnings this past week for everyone to be careful. As you know since my wife Esther passed away last year, I moved into a town house in the Historical District. Since it's a gated community with very good insulation, I guess I have been out of the loop on all of this.

Jennie told me that her "gang" chased these "mutant zombie freaks" (her words again) in streets and alleys. They pulled them from crawlspaces under cinder block foundations and shot them. They thought they had found almost all of those running loose until the temporary restraining order was served on her. That was why she came to our office. She saw that we had a large telephone pages ad and that we had been around longer than any other firm on the Island. She wants us to defend her against the lawsuit.

I can understand the skepticism likely expressed by my fellow partners at his juncture. However, she gave me a sixty thousand dollar retainer and agreed to a fee of three hundred an hour. At that rate, she could be a freak and I would consider defending her. Understand that this entire matter seems strange to me but her check cleared, so we'll enter an appearance in the case. I'll assign an associate to research the issues.

Angie. Please file this in Correspondence and Notes in the file. Note that you may need to fill in for Nance at reception today as she has apparently taken the rest of the day off. If you can find Jordan for me tell him that the filing is piling up. Walt

More News Clippings

NEWSWIRE
National Press
Galveston, Texas

Officials with the Texas National Guard have indicated that the Galveston Island quarantine will continue until further notice. The viral outbreak on the island has been reported to have infected a small but very violent number of persons on the island. In a related matter, a class action lawsuit has been filed in federal district court in Galveston County seeking injunctive relief from the hunting of persons infected with the virus. The petition asserts that deliberate and wanton hunting of these persons with the intent to kill them violates their rights under the equal protection clause of the 14th Amendment of the United States Constitution. A hearing on a preliminary injunction is set for next Tuesday.

NEWSWIRE
National Press
Galveston, Texas

The University of Galveston Medical Branch on Galveston Island has confirmed that twenty workers at the Infectious Research Center were infected by the so-called zombie virus. Through a Texas Open Records Request National Press was able to obtain copies of the exposure reports. Information on the virus itself was redacted on the grounds of national security. The remaining records indicate that the workers all exhibited violent behavior like the infected humans who had been reported to be attacking residents on the island. All but one of the workers was confined to treatment rooms at the hospital. The hospital also confirmed that Dr. Ira Dedin, one of the exposed workers and chief virologist at the hospital escaped from his confinement. Dedin was killed recently after an incident where he was found eating on a dog and attacked two policeman.

NEWSWIRE
National Press
Galveston, Texas

County Health Director Ignacio Farley announced today that the so-called "zombie virus" epidemic has been completely contained. "We have identified the remaining affected individuals and, God willing, we anticipate eliminating the last of them by the end of the week."

NEWSWIRE
National Press
Galveston, Texas

Federal District Judge Samuel B. DeMent has issued a preliminary injunction barring the hunting of infected persons still unaccounted for on the island. Citing legal precedence relating to the execution of incompetents Judge DeMent stated that the hunting and execution of infected persons was a violation of their constitutional rights. A final trial is set for later this summer. Royston Osteen of the Galveston County Sheriff's Department issued a statement that "The Sheriff's Department disagrees with the liberal social activism of Judge DeMent's ruling. However, the Department will obey the law and henceforth infected humans can no longer be shot on sight. Deputies will be instructed on the appropriate use of deadly force. God help us while we await the trial."

**IN THE UNITED STATES DISTRICT COURT
FOR THE COASTAL DISTRICT OF TEXAS
GALVESTON DIVISION**

John Doe, Zombie	§	
and all others similarly situated	§	**CAUSE NO. 2025-**
00666		
	§	
vs.	§	
	§	
Jennie Victim, ETAL	§	

**MEMORANDUM OPINION ON APPLICATION FOR
TEMPORARY INJUNCTION**

HON. SAMUEL B. DeMENT, PRESIDING:

Pending before this Court is a case of first impression but based on ancient law. Upon review of federal and state jurisprudence this Court is unable to find any identical proceeding of relevant precedential value. Due to the shortness of time and exigency of the circumstances, the Court will dispense with the typical discourse of the standard of review for preliminary injunctions in order to avoid a prolonged discussion.

Background of Dispute

This is a class action filed by a class of persons claiming to have been infected by a virus released from the University of Galveston Medical Branch on Galveston Island. This class has brought suit against the citizens of the island as a joint class. Class representative for the Plaintiff John Doe also euphemistically referred to in Plaintiff's pleadings as "John Doe Zombie" has filed a class action pursuant to Rule 23 of the Federal Rules of Civil Procedure. At the insistence of the Court in order to conclude the hearings before it, the parties have stipulated that the name "John Doe" or "John Doe Zombie" will be used to describe the plaintiff for the protection of the plaintiff and his family. Likewise, over the objections of plaintiff's counsel the lead defendant in this matter will also be referred to as Jennie Victim rather than her real name. These monikers have been set by the Court solely for purposes of protection from public identification and not to reflect a bias by the Court for either party. Also made parties to this suit are the University of Galveston Medical Branch, the City and County of Galveston and the State of Texas

The principal incidents giving rise to this matter occurred when this virus was apparently released by the University's Infectious Research Center. The origin of the virus is unknown and University officials, with the support of the United States Attorney General's office claimed national security prohibited its employees from testifying.

Civil discourse related to this viral release was first documented by reports of a Professor Ira Dedin attacking dogs on the east end of Galveston Island and devouring them raw and while still alive. When local police approached him he attacked two of them causing severe lacerations to their necks and arms with elongated nails and very sharp blackened teeth.

An hour later, the two policemen, while being treated for their wounds at the UGMB emergency room became agitated with a night nurse attempting to take blood samples. The policeman severely injured the nurse, disemboweling her while still alive. After being subdued, three more policemen and two orderlies were likewise bitten by this policeman. This appears to have begun a cycle of infections that eventually led to a small but actively violent throng of infected individuals roaming the streets of the island attacking homeowners.

After being rebuffed by a gang of vigilantes, the infected persons took to hiding. The gangs then grew, joined by local police and constables, and began to hunt down these infected persons and to kill them, the choice of killing being shooting the infected humans in the head severing their spinal cords from their brains. Testimony was given that these gangs have made a sport of these shootings going so far as to hold betting pools on "zombie headshots" giving cash awards to those with the highest kill rate on a given day. Some have even taken to using Japanese samurai katana blades to behead these infected humans. The island was placed on quarantine by the State enforced by the Texas State National Guard. Armed Guardsman began to assist these gangs bringing the full power of the state upon these stricken individuals.

The instant action was filed on behalf of these affected humans seeking injunctive relief against the citizens of the island, the county and the city and the State to prohibit the indiscriminate shooting and killing of these infected humans. Plaintiffs acknowledge that these infected humans are prone to extreme and bizarre bouts of violence and grotesque cannibalism. However, Plaintiffs allege that these individuals are in fact incompetent and as such are entitled to the protections under the law prohibiting cruel and unusual punishment as well as prohibiting the deprivation of life and liberty without due process at law. Plaintiffs also seek damages from the Defendants for injury caused to these infected humans. This Court concurs and grants the injunction.

Due Process Requirements Based on Evidence.

This Court acknowledges that in matters of civil unrest and discourse, the state may take actions, including the use of deadly force. Under state law, such matters are governed by Section 8 of the Texas Penal Code which provides, in part

Art. 8.04. DISPERSING RIOT. Whenever a number of persons are assembled together in such a manner as to constitute a riot, according to the penal law of the State, it is the duty of every magistrate or peace officer to cause such persons to disperse.   This may either be done by commanding them to disperse or by arresting the persons engaged, if necessary, either with or without warrant.

Art. 8.06. MEANS ADOPTED TO SUPPRESS. The officer engaged in suppressing a riot, and those who aid him are authorized and justified in adopting such measures as are necessary to suppress the riot, but are not authorized to use any greater degree of force than is requisite to accomplish that object.

Tex. Penal Code Ann. arts. 8.01, 8.04 and 8.06 (Vernon's). In the initial outbreak of this infection it was within the rights of the local authorities to use deadly force to suppress violent outbreaks when individual homes were invaded or individuals were attacked in the streets. Texas law would even exonerate those who "shoot to kill" too quickly injuring or killing innocent bystanders under the mistaken belief that they are rioters. This is consistent with longstanding law in many jurisdictions. For example, in the case of Courvoisier v. Raymond, 23 Colo. 113, 47 P. 284 (Colo.1896) the Colorado Supreme Court held that if during a riot one believes his life is in danger he is justified in using self-defense, even against an innocent victim, if he reasonably believes that the victim posed an immediate danger to him. However, once the riot had spent itself, and thus the immediate threat ended, a different situation arose.

This Court received testimony from a distinguished fellow in medicine. Dr. Pedigrew Lipmoss, neurologist with the Caylor Medical School in Harrison County testified that unlike so-called "zombies" of movie lore, as these persons were described by the Texas Attorney General, these infected humans were neither undead nor reanimated. They were living human beings infected by a virus which could potentially be cured given time. Dr. Lipmoss even suggested that the passage of time could potentially allow the virus to be successfully fought by the immune system and these individuals become normal again; that is, if not recklessly murdered for their mere status as infected persons. Thus, these persons are not "zombies" as the State, City and County would assert. They are citizens afflicted with a disease that has rendered them incompetent and thus not responsible for even the most violent of their own actions.

The County attempted to present testimony of their health director, Ignacio Farley. Mr. Farley, who has no actual medical background but rather a degree in inorganic biology, suggested that the virus could mutate so as to become airborne. Thus, he reasoned, the safety of the public at large dictated the actions of the State, City and County in hunting down these affected individuals. Mr. Farley's testimony is, however, nothing more than unproven junk science which does not meet the standards set out by the Supreme Court in Daubert v. Merrell Dow Pharmaceuticals, 509 U.S. 579 (1993). As such, his testimony has been stricken from the record and was not considered.

As noted above, this is a case of first impression. However, the Court takes judicial notice of a plethora of historical abuses wherein the rights of the incompetent or those unable to defend themselves have been violated. The history of the United States is replete with race riots against African-Americans, hate crimes against women and homosexuals and even the wholesale internment of a people based on race and nationality- those of Japanese descent. In Dusky v. United States, 362 U.S. 402 (1960) (per curiam), the Supreme Court held that every individual is entitled to a competency evaluation before proceeding to trial. Why then would the Eighth Amendment's prohibition against cruel and unusual punishment allow for the wholesale slaughter of infected humans based solely on their status as an incompetent? See Robinson v. California, 370 U.S. 660 (1962) (states cannot make status alone a crime). A defendant declared incompetent cannot even be held indefinitely. There must be a showing that the individual will ultimately become competent to be tried or else they must be released. Jackson v. Indiana 406 U.S. 715 (1972). Persons judged incompetent or insane cannot be subjected to the death penalty. Ford v. Wainwright, 477 U.S. 399 (1986). Thus, the execution, summary or otherwise, of a citizen rendered incompetent due to this infection would constitute cruel and unusual punishment.

The actions of the Defendants are so beyond the pale as to shock the conscious of this Court. The Sheriff of Galveston County attempted to testify that their actions were justified because the mere presence of these unfortunates slowly ambling down the narrow Galveston streets constituted an "inherent threat to the safety and well-being of the public." He admitted that generally they were fairly easy to avoid when encountered in the street if not in large numbers stating, "Yeah, you can get away from them pretty easy, but if you want to kill them you have to get up real close to shoot them in the head. You want a clean shot either blowing out their brains or severing the spinal cord."

The Sheriffs own testimony indicated a severe bias and ill intent when he stated on the record that "We can't have these types just wandering around. We had to do something or our whole way of life would have been threatened." He then again admitted that the infection caused them to move very slowly. They were easy to spot, he boasted, which made them much easier to shoot. This cowboy movie mentality is not frontier justice; it is state sponsored murder.

Would he have said the same of a congregation of paraplegics in wheelchairs? Or brain injured individuals or Alzheimer's patients? Would it be acceptable to wager on "headshots" of the mentally disabled? And if so, how much of a stretch of a "sense of threat" would it be to slaughter illegal immigrants quietly walking to take their stations at the menial, demeaning jobs relegated to them due to their mere status or African-American teenagers walking home from the store. The rights of the less fortunate cannot be so cavalieristically twisted to justify murderous bigotry at the meanest and most abhorrent of levels; the taking of the lives of humans incapable of self-defense due to their mere status.

While normally governmental entities of the state of Texas would be entitled to sovereign immunity, that immunity does not apply to the violation of the civil rights of individuals. Accordingly the motions to dismiss filed by the City and County of Galveston and the State of Texas are hereby denied. However, the University of Galveston Medical Branch, in conjunction with briefing from the United States Attorney's Office revealed in sealed documents that the research at the Infectious Research Center was cloaked in national security and thus, despite the gross injustice of the result and disemboweling of fairness, the claims against the University are dismissed.

Conclusion

The Court finds, based on the available evidence, that the practice of hunting down and killing of infected humans, solely due to their status, violates the tenants of the U.S. Constitution and their rights as citizens. Because of this, the Court finds that the Plaintiffs have a reasonably foreseeable chance of succeeding in their claims, lack an adequate remedy at law and thus are entitled to injunctive relief against the wholesale and government sanctioned slaughter of infected individuals. The State of Texas and the City and County will present briefing and testimony as to the proper and humane capture and containment of these individuals, subject to the contempt powers of this Court. Trial of this matter shall be set at a hearing to be determined in the future.

Judge Presiding

Depositions

CAUSE NO. 2027-•00666

John Doe, Zombie	) IN THE UNITED STATES DISTRICT COURT
and all others similarly situated	)
	) FOR THE
	)
vs.	) COASTAL DISTRICT
	)
Jennie Victim,	)
ET AL	) GALVESTON DIVISION

****

ORAL DEPOSITION Jennie Victim
VOLUME I of I

****

ORAL DEPOSITION OF Jennie Victim, produced as a witness at the instance of the Plaintiff and duly sworn, was taken in the above-styled and numbered cause on from 1:36 p.m. to 3:09 p.m., before Lisa Shothand, Certified Shorthand Reporter in and for the State of Texas, reported by computerized stenotype machine at the offices of FLEXTON AND ASSOCIATES 200 SABER, HOUSTON, TX 77009, pursuant to the Federal Rules of Civil Procedure and the provisions stated on the record or attached hereto.

APPEARANCES FOR THE PLAINTIFF:

MR. MAURINCE FLEXTONE
FLEXTON AND ASSOCIATES
200 SABER
HOUSTON, TX 77009
Telephone: SUPPRESSED BY COURT ORDER
Fax: SUPPRESSED BY COURT ORDER

FOR THE DEFENDANT JENNIE VICTIM

WALTER WALKER JOHNSON:
JOHNSON, JONES & RABINOWITZ
802 LOCKENDOWN GALVESTON, TX
Telephone: SUPPRESSED BY COURT ORDER
Fax: SUPPRESSED BY COURT ORDER

FOR THE DEFENDANT CITY AND COUNTY OF GALVESTON TEXAS:

MS. MADISON LARUE ORSEY
COUNTY ATTORNEY'S OFFICE
802 LOCKENDOWN GALVESTON, TX
Telephone: SUPPRESSED BY COURT ORDER
Fax: SUPPRESSED BY COURT ORDER

JENNIE VICTIM, having been first duly sworn, testified as follows:
EXAMINATION

Q   (BY MR. FLEXTON)   MS. VICTIM, would you state your name for the record, please, sir?

A   My name is JENNIE VICTIM.

Q   Okay, M'am. Is that your real name?

A.   No, of course not. You're the ones who sued me and what's left of my family remember?

Q.   And where do you live?

A   Your clients know where I live. They ate my husband and two of my children.

MR. FLEXTONE: Objection, Nonresponsive.

Q   (BY MR. FLEXTON   M'am, isn't it true that you have lived at 2828 Mockingbird Lane since 1982?

A   Yes, sir, that's where I used to live.

Q   What do you do, M'am?

A   Before, or after the freaks started to come out?

MR. FLEXTONE: Objection, Nonresponsive, argumentative and improper sidebar.

MR. JOHNSON: Maury. Give her a break. Your clients ate her kids and now you want to know where she's been hiding out?

MR. FLEXTONE: Walter, I'm going to have to object to that sidebar too. Everyone knows that my clients did not have the mental capacity as infected humans –

MR. JOHNSON: You mean zombies.

MR. FLEXTONE: We're not going to take this abuse from you folks. The court has already sanctioned your client twice for refusing to appear for her deposition. Do we have to get another ruling on this?

MR. JOHNSON: She didn't want to be eaten. She had good cause. She knew you'd have one of those infected things here today.

MR. FLEXTONE: The Court didn't agree, now can we move on please?

Q   (BY MR. FLEXTON)   MS. VICTIM, You do understand that you are here regarding a class action filed by my client and all other similarly infected humans who were shot by you and the other defendants in violation of their civil rights?

A   They tried to eat us. We had no choice. I do not regret shooting the bastards. I do not regret pulling people together to go after them, even my own husband when he started showing the infection.

MR. FLEXTONE: Objection, Nonresponsive.

Q   (BY MR. FLEXTON)   MS. VICTIM, the court has already ruled from the bench that my client and the others were not mentally competent and as such were not responsible for their actions.

MR. JOHNSON: Objection, mischaracterizing the evidence and the court's ruling. Your clients may have been out of their minds, but that didn't mean they didn't deserve what they got and you know that.

MR. FLEXTON: The court ruled otherwise in his order didn't he? You also know that the court has set this for trial on the issue of damages and we are not going to re-litigate any other issues.

MR. JOHNSON: We are appealing that motion.

Q   (BY MR. FLEXTON: Well, good luck on that. Ms., er, Victim, I want to take you to the night in question that led to your organizing thugs to hunt down my clients.

(witness sobs)

Q   (BY MR. FLEXTON: MS. VICTIM, do we need to take a break already? (witness nods)

Q   (BY MR. FLEXTON: MS. VICTIM, were you and your family at home that night.

A   Yes.

Q   (BY MR. FLEXTON: Describe for the jury please how it came to be that you deliberately shot my client and his companions.

A   They ate my kids and tried to eat my husband so I shot them. I had to shoot him too later you know. Do you think I enjoyed that? What they did was horrible. I still have nightmares from it. I shot them and I will hunt them down until they eat the eyeballs from my sockets before I stop hunting them.

[End of Transcript]

Henson & Associates, P.C.
18000 Louisiana
Suite 5500
Houston, Texas 77005

Walter William Johnson   Via Facsimile
Johnson, Jones & Rabinowitz
802 Lockendown
Galveston, Texas

Walt:

Please consider this letter our last formal cease and desist to your client Jennie "Victim." Contrary to the preliminary injunction issued by the Honorable Samuel B. DeMent your client attended her deposition yesterday with the obvious intent to cause bodily harm to the attending class representative at her deposition. We were not able to go beyond twenty minutes into her deposition when your client decided to brandish a firearm, to wit a so-called "sawed-off shotgun," and proceeded to shoot the class representative in the head and then the court reporter. Your client's assertion that she was defending herself is completely fallacious. Your client was not attacked by the class representative nor directly threatened by him. Brandishing a firearm of this nature after concealing it in a large, oversized hand bag at a deposition taken pursuant to both the Rules of Civil Procedure and Court order is inexcusable. We will seek severe sanctions and the cost expended by my firm to secure the class representative at the depositions. It took us several days to find and properly secure him so he could be there. We will ask Judge DeMent to strike your pleadings entering a judgment against your clients and the remaining Defendants.

Your immediate attention to this matter is demanded.

Regards,

Maury

Maurice "Maury" Flextone
For the Firm

Memorandum To: The Partners of the Firm

From: *WWJ*

Re: Doe v. Victim- Deposition of Jennifer
Watson

As you can see from the attached letter, the deposition did
not go well. I did not know that Jennie was packing when
she came in. She had assured me that she did not come
prepared to hurt anyone. In her defense, I have to say that
she was provoked. The letter may be superficially accurate
that she was not directly threatened by the class
representative. She expressed her objection on the record to
his attendance. Maury just as viscerally responded that the
basic rule of law is that the client can attend the deposition.
Maury is correct on the Rules of course, but he was supposed
to keep him at bay. The thing was disgusting. His eyes were
like red centers floating in yellow ich. While his skin did not
appear to be rotting, it was severely cracked throughout and
dripped through the cloth of his coveralls. And the smell;
that god-awful smell.

We managed to get through some basics when Jennie
admitted that she shot the original "John Doe Zombie" after
the thing attacked her kids and husband and were eating on
them. She also admitted that she helped form a gang of men
and women to hunt down the remaining infected humans on
the Island. She even admitted that she enjoyed shooting them
down as they ambled toward her. She admitted that the sole
reason she shot them was because of what they were - the
infected things that killed her family members. She even
hunted down her own husband who had apparently become
infected as well. The class representative appeared to be
unfocused and staring at the court reporter; a lovely girl I

have used before but forget her name right off hand. I thought everything was okay, except of course for Jennie's admissions. However, the so-called "class representative" got out of his bindings and attacked the court reporter, not Jennie. To my shock, Jennie pulled out her weapon and shot the man in the head, cleanly separating his skull from his spinal cord. She then looked at the bleeding court reporter and watched as her skin began to boil with blisters and cysts and begin to crack. When the reporter's teeth turned black Jennie shot her too. Maury was hiding under the table. Jennie grabbed her bag, smiled at me and left. The letter followed shortly. I expect a motion for sanctions to be filed and as we all know Judge DeMent is going to go off the deep end on this one. We'll have to take one of the prettier associates with us which may at least temper his appetite for blood while satisfying others.

We still have $30,000 in the trust fund for the retainer. When that is used up, we'll withdraw.

NEWSWIRE
National Press
Galveston, Texas.

The Texas Department of Public Safety has issued an "infected persons" warning to all residents of the following counties: Galveston, Harris, Matagorda, Chambers and Montgomery. The warning will remain in effect until further notice. Residents are advised to keep indoors during periods of high activity and are reminded that the federal courts have ruled that the deliberate hunting down and stalking of "infected persons" is prohibited. You may only use deadly force in the event of a direct home invasion by these persons. Local police and sheriffs offices have been advised to implement proper use of deadly force protocols when engaging these persons.

NEWSWIRE
National Press
Muncie, Indiana

The National Firearms Association has begun advertising the
sale of "Zombie Target Dummies" which are life-sized
mannequins "zombified" to appear to be an infected human.
The Association's press release announcing the new product
line claimed that the targets are designed to help citizens
properly target "zombies" and comes with an electronic
scoring system for severing limbs and "headshots" resulting
in the severing of the skull from the body. "It's great fun for
the family and educational too," said a telemarketer hired by
the Association who asked not to be named or otherwise
identified.

NEWSWIRE
National Press
Galveston, Texas.

Judge Samuel B. DeMent has issued another ruling making
his prior injunction against the hunting of "infected persons"
even more sweeping. He granted summary judgment in favor
of the class action plaintiffs that they should be considered
incompetent and thus cannot be subjected to capital
punishment. He also struck the pleadings of the defendants
for what he called "horrendous actions showing utter
disregard and disrespect for this Court and the Constitution"
due to evidence of continued "'zombie hunts" and shootings
of class representatives during depositions. The Defendants
said that they would appeal.

IN THE UNITED STATES COURT OF APPEALS FOR THE COASTAL CIRCUIT

No. 25-20266
Summary Calendar

JENNIFER VICTIM AND
ALL THOSE SIMILARLY SITUATED
AS DEFENDANTS, ET AL.

Plaintiff-Appellee v.

JOHN DOE ZOMBIE
AND ALL THOSE SIMILARLY SITUATED
PLAINTIFFS,

Defendant-Appellant

Before Garnstone, Chief Judge, and Winken and Kissamee, Circuit Judges.

PER CURIAM:

The Majority of the En Bane Panel, upon review of the Emergency Appeal of Appellee Jennie Victim finds no abuse of discretion in the rulings of the trial court. Accordingly, the appeal is dismissed and the rulings of the trial court are AFFIRMED.

----

* Pursuant to 5TH CIR. R. 47.5, the court has determined that this opinion should not be published and

is not precedent except under the limited circumstances set forth in 5TH CIR. R. 47.5.4.

Correspondence and Notes

Memorandum To: The Partners of the Firm

From: *WWJ*

Re: Appeals Court Ruling

The Appeals Court lost a transistor and didn't even give us oral argument on the emergency appeal. They weren't impressed that Judge DeMent has not returned to the bench after his ruling for improprieties with his secretaries. I suppose it was one thing to try to force his head between their legs, we all knew he was rather abusive to those gals, but when he started to bite they complained and the U.S. Marshall's office put six bullets in him before he escaped from the court house. I would guess he's out there somewhere wandering the streets like the other freaks. The client has collected another $50,000 from neighbors and wired it into the trust account. The problem we are going to have on appeal, I told the client, was that Judge DeMent limited the record and even cross examination. I told her that federal judges are the "closest thing to God on earth." We all know about that, especially him. I still go in there with a tooth brush in my pocket in case he tries to find me in contempt again for calling '"sir" instead of "Judge" like that one time. With that kind of record, the Supreme Court may simply decide there's nothing to review.

Jennie has not helped the situation either. She says that she had three more encounters near her new home and is finally giving up on the island if she and her friends have to live with these infected "freaks" as she call them. I have explained to her that she can't hunt down these people indiscriminately. Even before the injunction, Texas gun laws were very clear. If they go on her property at night, she can shoot them. If they go on her neighbor's property at night, she can shoot them. If they are on her property or her neighbor's property at night, she has to shoot them before they cross back over the property line into the street. If they are on the street walking around, even if looking threatening, she can't shoot them unless they actually attack someone and that attack is unprovoked. If it's daytime, even if they stray onto her property she has to wait until they appear to threaten her to shoot them so she can invoke "Stand Your Ground." I also reminded her that even though Texas is a "'pro-gun" state, you have to have a permit to walk around with a concealed gun. Without a permit, the gun has to be out in the open and she has to be going to or from her home or place of business or making a run to the bank. Otherwise, I told her, she could be arrested. She told me she would take that into consideration. I doubt she listened.

On a sadder note, I regret to inform you that our longstanding paralegal Gladys was killed last night by a neighbor. The facts are still murky but it seems that the neighbor claims that Gladys, still in those ugly gray sweatpants and top she liked to wear to the office, was in her back yard with her husband. At first the neighbor thought Gladys was engaging in some type of alternative sex act with him when the neighbor realized that her husband's body parts in Gladys's mouth were no longer attached to her husband so the neighbor shot her. I am not sure if this means that Gladys's Estate will join the putative class of Plaintiffs which could cause us to be disqualified from this case.

However, I am hoping the Supremes accept our emergency appeal and we get some sanity in this situation.

.NEWSWIRE
National Press
Washington, D.C.

The United States Supreme Court has conditionally granted review of the emergency appeal filed on behalf of the Defendants in the so-called "Zombie Appeal" based on the acceptance of the appeal by Justices Scatalagia and Calisto, generally considered the two most conservative judges on the court. However, the court declined to lift the implementation of the injunction issued by the late Judge Samuel B. Dement, formerly federal district judge in Galveston.

In an unrelated matter, rumors as to the whereabouts of Justice Briar have been circulating. The often "swing vote" on the court has not reported to work for several days and rumors as to his status as an "infected person" have been denied by his press secretary.

Reports of "zombie" outbreaks now appear to be transnational with riots breaking out in Hong Kong. Citizens can be seen engaging in everyday activities wearing surgical masks and gloves to avoid infection, and carrying large knives and other long blades for protection.

NEWSWIRE
National Press
Washington, D.C.

Dr. Bradford T. Mainard of Southern Baptist University's medical school issued a paper this afternoon claiming that he had been able to isolate the genetic markers affected by the so-called "zombie virus." Dr. Mainard claims in his paper that due to the apparently artificial manipulation of the DNA of the virus, persons falling into the following categories are the least likely to be affected by the virus: sexually active homosexuals; sexually active female teens on birth control pills; heavy smokers of marijuana and male African Americans between the ages of 12 and 27. Dr. Mainard stated that his work was based on blood samples and case studies. The University's governing board immediately disavowed the study claiming it to be unconfirmed hyperbole and against Biblical instruction.

Former University President and evangelist, Deacon P. Gray, once known for his virulent anti-gay campaigns until he was outed for late night trysts with male prostitutes issued a press release shortly thereafter stating, "I was only following God's mysterious plan." A spokesperson for the National Firearms Association called the new study "proof of a left-wing conspiracy to destroy and undermine the moral fabric of our society."

A poll of major corporations in the Houston area indicated that none appeared willing to alter drug-free work rules as a result of this scientific paper.

Memorandum To: All Employees

From: *WWJ*

Re: Office Hours and Procedures

It has come to my attention that there are rumors within the office that we will be closing the Galveston office. These rumors are completely untrue. We certainly understand the concerns you have regarding crossing the causeway and having to undergo blood tests periodically given by surly National Guardsman wearing chemical protective gear. This office has been a landmark of this island for over 40 years and we don't intend to change that. For those who work down here we do not have room for you in the Houston office so do not report to work there please or you may have your hours docked. If you don't come to work, you won't have a job.

I have also been advised by some members of the staff that certain people have been using derogatory descriptions of the class action plaintiffs in our "John Doe" appeal. You are advised that we are an equal opportunity employer and will not tolerate such things. The use of the "Z" word is not allowed any time at this office.

Memorandum To: The Partners of the Firm

From: *WWJ*

Re: Zombie Appeal

I have just been advised that Mr. Flextone will not be appearing at the Supreme Court for tomorrow's oral argument. His office indicated that he had some '"client control" issues and they have engaged local counsel in Washington, D.C. They would not elaborate as to where Flextone was or whether he would be returning to his office. I am flying out there tonight.

Some of you have expressed concern regarding the billing on this matter and rest assured that the bill is current and up to date. However, the trust fund balance will likely be exhausted after the oral argument tomorrow

Memorandum To: The Partners of the Firm

From: *WWJ*

Re: Banana Docks, Inc

Our clients Banana Docks, Inc. called me this morning and they have shut down operations until further notice. Apparently, they attempted to bring in extra help, after experiencing such high absenteeism, but attempted to use workers from Union Hall No. 37 out of Rockport. The local union put up picket signs and the replacement workers would not cross the lines. I guess the fact that a group of the picketers turned out to be infected persons who attacked the Rockport union members didn't help. They say they will bring their billing current in the near future.

Memorandum To: The Partners of the Firm

From: *WWJ*

Re: Business Development

The publicity from the current "John Doe" or "Zombie" Appeal (yes I know what I told the staff but this is just between us), has been very positive. I have personally been asked to appear on Badger News Network along with representatives of the National Firearms Association to discuss the rights of homeowners. I have been approached by three of the local refineries to help set up policies on random blood testing for infected persons.

Ira has been promoting a new legal product he calls the "Living Dead Will." It is a legal document to place your assets in a trust in case you become an infected person and directing the trustee of your trust to hire persons to find you and secure you until a cure can be found. Apparently, several of the old families in town have requested some sort of protection in this event and Ira thinks it can fly through the probate courts if needed. Once recorded it will allow the families to quietly, without publicity, sequester their own family member to protect them from gangs.

NEWSWIRE
National Press
Austin, Texas.

The Texas Attorney General announced today that the U.S. Supreme Court has agreed to allot time for him to address the court as a '"friend of the court" or amicus participant. Attorney General Kronen said that he intended to "bring the justices to Jesus" and have them understand the situation in Texas. Blaming what he called the "Maim Stream Media" for unwarranted sympathy for the so-called "infected persons", Attorney General Kronen also urged the Texas legislature to pass the "Voter Blood ID Bill" co-authored by several state representatives. "We can't have these infected folks trying to vote in our elections and skewing the will of the people while trying to kill them at the same time. We have to protect our way of life down here."

Attorney General Kronen's office also stated that they are still waiting for a response to their request allowing the attorneys presenting oral argument to be armed in the event the crowds of protestors expected outside of the Supreme Court Building show signs of infection

Supreme Court Transcript and Ruling

IN THE SUPREME COURT OF THE UNITED

STATES

- - - -

JENNIE VICTIM,ET AL.

Petitioners   No. 27-989

v.

JOHN DOE ZOMBIE, ET AL.

Respondents

- - - - - - -

Washington, D.C.
The above-entitled matter came on for
oral argument before the Supreme Court
of the United States at 10:12 a.m.
APPEARANCES:

WALTER WALKER JOHNSON, GALVESTON, TX;
on behalf of Petitioners, JENNIE VICTIM,
ET AL..

DARRYL J. BASTINI., Washington, D.C.; on
behalf of Respondents, JOHN DOE ZOMBIE,
ET AL.

HON. ARTHUR F. KRONEN, ESQ., AUSTIN,
TX.;
on behalf of Respondents STATE OF TEXAS,
CITY AND COUNTY OF GALVESTON, TEXAS AND
INDIVIDUALLY AS AMICUS PARTICIPANT

P R O C E E D I N G S

(10:12 a.m.)

CHIEF JUSTICE COGDEN: We will hear
argument this morning in Case Number 27-
989, Jennie Victim et al. v. John Doe
Zombie, et al.

Mr. Johnson.

ORAL ARGUMENT OF WALTER WALKER JOHNSON
FOR PETITIONERS

MR. JOHNSON: Mr. Chief Justice, and may
it please the Court:

This is a case that has elevated from a
local injunction proceeding to one that
now goes to the very core of the
personal safety and security of all
Americans. News reports of attacks by
these virally infected, flesh eating
humans are commonplace from Galveston to
New York City to Paris, France. At the
outset Petitioners recognize that the
record before this Distinguished Court
is sparse. But that is only due to the
determined effort of the trial court-

JUSTICE Ginblossom: The Court of
Appeals found no error on the part of
the apparently late Judge DeMent in his
handling of the hearing on the

preliminary injunction. They also found no error in his striking your client's pleadings. Why should that be a matter of discussion here? Or, are you suggesting we go outside the record?

MR. JOHNSON: The trial record and the reality of the situation would seem to mandate that this Court review what has happened since that hearing. None of us had any idea that this viral outbreak would become a world-wide calamity. The evidence regarding the airborne nature of the virus rejected by the trial court is also now proven to be accurate. We beseech this Court to look outside the record of the trial court so that justice may be served.

JUSTICE MONTEMOYER: Well, that depends,-- as the Respondent points out, a Rule 54(b) motion for rehearing was never filed with the trial court. Wouldn't that have been prudent to have done. You could do that now.

MR. JOHNSON: Judge DeMent began to show symptoms of the virus himself within a few weeks of his ruling. It was then that the airborne nature of the virus began to manifest itself. If this Court wishes to admonish my failings as a counselor, so be it, but please do not allow that to ---

JUSTICE SCATALIGA: Are you all
infected? There are zombies just outside
our doors now. Who knows where Justice
Briar is. This is a disaster, we can't
allow legalistic rules overcome common
sense. Even socialist Sweden has been
arming its citizens.

JUSTICE MONTEMOYER: Are you suggesting
then

PAGE3

that this Court abandon your
longstanding refusal to allow this Court
to review matters beyond American
jurisprudence? I think we need a
definitive stance.

JUSTICE SCATALIGA: Of course not. It is
improper to use foreign law to determine
the meaning of the Constitution.

MR. JOHNSON: If I may interject, this
is a matter of the lives of millions.

CHIEF JUSTICE COGDEN: But that is
what judges do every day counselor and
given that we are appointed for life we
get a long time to do it in. The one
constant is our rules. You suggest we
bend our rules, our procedures, for
nothing more than the crisis flavor of
the month. Rules need to be respected.

(inaudible screams from the audience)

CHIEF JUSTICE COGDEN: Order. We do
not allow outbursts from the audience.
One more and I will have the U.S.
Marshalls clear the gallery.

(inaudible screams).

CHIEF JUSTICE COGDEN: I have just been
advised by Marshalls that the doors have
been breached by infected humans and we
have to clear the room. This matter will
adjourned.

UNKNOWN SPEAKER: Oh my God, it's Justice
Briar.

(inaudible. shots fired)

UNKNOWN SPEAKER: The Texas Attorney
General just shot Justice Briar's head
off.

NEWSWIRE
National Press
Washington, D.C.

In a 4-4 decision, the United States Supreme Court has effectively upheld the ruling of the Coastal Circuit Court of Appeals refusing to lift the injunction against the hunting of infected persons.

Justice Montemoyer, writing for the traditional liberal 4 members of the Court, noted that the weak trial record left it no choice but to find no error in the injunction. The four justices stated that the Constitution protected the rights of all citizens and this included discrimination due to status even when due to health concerns, such as infected persons. To hold otherwise, Montemoyer ruled, would be an affront to the core of the Constitution.

Justice Scatalgia writing for the 4 traditionally conservative justices stated that he no longer cared what the Constitution says. "I just don't want to die," he wrote in a cryptic opinion he claimed was written while barricaded in his chambers while two of his law clerks ate his long time secretary. "She was faithful to the end," a spokesperson for Justice Scatalagia stated in a written press release.

Meanwhile, Congress was unable, after ten votes, to overcome filibusters blocking the President's nomination of Texas Attorney General Kronen to replace Justice Briar on the U.S. Supreme Court. Rumors that the President has been relocated to a sealed bunker in the Appalachians were denied by the sole member of the President's staff who could be located today.

Memorandum To: All Employees
From: *Samual P. Jones*
Re: Office Hours and Procedures.

It has come to my attention that employees are not reporting to work at 8:00 a.m. sharp as set out in our Firm manual. I don't have to remind you that this firm traces its roots to the very first law firm licensed in the state of Texas. We did not get to be here this long by letting rules go to the wayside during hard times.

We start work at 8:00 a.m. sharp. We will dock your pay if you are late.

Firm Associates are expected to turn in their time sheets to their secretaries each morning so the time can be entered on our billing system. We can't let that go to the wayside either.

For those employees who have not shown up for work this past week claiming illness, you will not be paid. The Family Medical Leave Act does not apply to this office because we are too small, so arguments to the contrary will not be considered.

However, the one change in protocol we will allow is that all employees will be allowed to maintain concealed weapons on their persons while at work even if they do not have a permit issued by the State of Texas. As a show of support for Firm morale, the Firm has purchased ammunition which will be stored in the supply room. Please understand that bullets and shotgun shells are expensive and these are not items to be taken home to your children for school. Please advise our new office manager of any special orders required.

Also, someone continues to leave food in the form of small rodents and animals out in the parking lot. I understand some of you may have relatives out there and are worried about them. However, this is creating an unsightly mess every morning and it should stop.

We also acknowledge the current medical statements issued by the U.S. Center for Infectious Diseases advising employers to encourage prophylactic lifestyle measures to attempt to enhance the immune system. However, we remain a smoke-free building until further notice and remind you that we do not have locks on inner doors and any inappropriate behavior discovered by your supervisors will subject you to discipline up to and including termination of your employment.

And please refrain from shooting co-workers in the building. If you suspect that a co-worker has been infected you are to bring the matter to your supervisor pursuant to Firm policy and, if needed, the employee will be escorted from the building with the standard two weeks severance.

Finally, it is with deep regret that I have to announce that Mr. Johnson has left the Firm. Last I was told, he left the office last Tuesday and has not returned here or to his home since. If he appears at the door please only open fire on him if he tries to open it. Remember, there is an injunction still pending.

Black Friday
by Willy Adkins

The cool air bristled across the wide open space of the dimly lit parking lot. The sun was still a long ways away. It was just a very faded light blue haze on the distant horizon. Most nights, it would be the dead time of night, with the world still asleep, but that night, that morning, it was far from still and asleep. Not the early pre-dawn morning after Thanksgiving.

Cars and trucks filled with holiday travelled shoppers roamed in the early morning streets. Coffee shops were already opened to the morning participants and filled with many people getting their refills. Family members would be switching out from the long lines as many would be tucked away in their vehicles while one member would brave the cold. Solitary shoppers would be heavily bundled with hunter hand warmers placed strategically throughout their body to attempt to keep them warm.

Winter was coming, and so was Christmas.

Tim stood there. He was one of the many shoppers getting ready to storm the doors into the closed department store. The store itself still had an hour before they would open to the onslaught of customers and the line outside was already stretched around to the side of the building, it's end lost out of sight. He was glad that he was one of the few people closest to the door, but then he had also been camping there since before the store had even closed the night before.

"I'm going back to the car."

Tim looked over his shoulder. Michelle was shivering behind him. Her face, the little he could see exposed as most of it was hidden behind her pink scarf, was pale white from the cold. Even her normally bright blue eyes seemed to be iced over with a sheen of frost. He had warned her beforehand about coming with him that it wasn't easy to stand in the lines for hours on end. She had thought it would be fun. She could play on her phone and text people, she had told him. That had lasted fifteen minutes. By midnight, she had already been complaining about wanting to go home and come back later.

She didn't understand.

"Okay hun. You go get yourself warmed up." He said to her. She hadn't even waited for him. She had already turned and was bouncing back to their little Ford Escort. The heat wouldn't kick on for a couple minutes if it did at all, but she had blankets in there and it would get her out of the wind.

The couple next to him really came prepared. They were seated in lawn chairs, large, thick blankets pulled up to their faces, and full head gear to keep them warm. They had long since fallen asleep, and were statues to the God of greed.

Others nearby had set up tents. Those were the fanatics. They had been camped out there for two days. When Tim first showed up, he couldn't help but find out more, like what they were there for. One of them was just there for the event of it. He just planned on picking up a couple of new DVD's.

Michelle was shocked by the madness of it all. She was furious as first. "Didn't any of these people have families they should be with? It's Thanksgiving!?"

Tim just smiled. She was cute.

That she was, in her tight blue jeans that sometimes looked like they were just painted on. A wiggle fit, he called them, as he knew she had to shake her booty viciously to fit them into the small space of the pants. Then there was her slim fitting sweater that was thick enough to be warm, but still tight to her shape.

Damn he felt lucky having her there with him, even if she did spend most the time in the car.

Tim looked back behind him. People were still pulling into the parking lot and crossing over towards the distant end of the line. The stream was becoming larger, more cars were driving on the roads, and the morning was waking up in greater force.

He loved being out there for it. Just the feeling of being a part of the morning as it was waking up. The air smelled different. The cool breeze felt different. Like it was electric, pulsating intensely in preparation to what was to come.

Tim scanned the parking lot, at how the morning was coming alive, and stopped when his gaze fell upon his car. He watched as the exhaust created a small poisonous fog spitting out from the rusted tailpipe.

Maybe he should think about getting a new car instead of waiting in line for a television.

That exhaust had to be filtering into the heat. He didn't know how she could stand to just sit in there. Then again, it was either that or out here in the cold. Just like her good looks, she would nearly die if it meant to keep herself comfortable or looking good.

Tim shifted as he noticed that she wasn't alone in the car. She was sitting behind the wheel, but Tim could just make out another shape sitting there with her. He couldn't see it too well, but there was definitely a dark shape moving around in the front seat of the car. It was making the whole car shake rocking back and forth. If Tim hadn't known better, he would have thought that there was sexual feeling going on, but Michelle would never, and it was too soon after she had left.

Tim didn't stop to think about his place in line when the driver's side door opened and he could hear her screaming. Michelle's scream could be heard loudly throughout the parking lot and it chilled him even deeper. He tried to run as fast as he could, but his legs had long since gone numb from standing and being out there in the cold. They burned and pulled against him.

He neared the car, as Michelle was trying to pull herself out. Her hands just reaching over the top of the door were covered in blood, and she struggled against the dark shape, trying to pull herself away. He could hear her, struggling, sounding like she was trying to kick herself away, but with the windows fogged, and the angle he had ran towards her, he still couldn't see much more than the streaks of blood coming down the driver's side door.

"Michelle!" Tim yelled. He could see in greater detail how the passenger side window had been broken in, and the dark shape was reaching through from the other side, chasing after his girlfriend.

She was staring at him through the window as some of the fog had started to fade, making her face just a haze. Her expression was of desperation, and he knew that tears were streaming down her face. He tried to push himself even faster, to get around the door to get to her.

"Michelle!"

He rounded around the open door, quickly reaching in to grab for her hand.

"Take my hand!" Tim said. He reached for hers, but she wouldn't grab it. Her grip remained tight on the door, fingers locked into their grasp. Her skin was covered in blood and he grabbed at her hands to pull them away. Her fingers stayed locked. She refused to look at him, and a lump was beginning to form in the pit of his stomach. There was a lot of blood. He hoped like hell that it wasn't hers. He silently prayed to himself that it wasn't.

He finally was able to break away her fingers from the frame, and took her hands into his. The blood was wet and sticky, and he had to fight to keep hold of her as he started pulling her out of the front seat of the car. She wrenched back, pulled away from him when her hand broke free from the door frame.

He had to pull harder. A tug of war occurred with Michelle being used as rope. He pulled with all of his strength coursing through his legs to dig into the blacktop of the parking lot. The shape, hidden in the darkness of the car, Tim couldn't see who, or what had her, he just knew he wanted to get Michelle away from it. He pulled, harder, feeling as she was starting to come farther from the front seat of the car. Then with a sudden snap, she was broken free and lunged forward towards him.

He fell back, and Michelle came crashing down on top of him. Blood was dripping from her, and he could see the large chunk of flesh taken out of her neck. He could also see her collar bone right where skin and muscle should have been through a large rip in her sweater. Around the tear, a massive amount of red crimson already drenched her sweater around the gaping hole and it was quickly getting worse.

Tim looked to her eyes, turning her face so that she was looking at him. Her face turned, but her eyes were barely open, and looked at him with a blank gaze. Her mouth was open, but inside, her tongue flopped with the motion as Tim was jerking her around, trying to get her to snap out of it. She was gone.

He let her go, and started to pull himself out from under her. His eyes stayed locked into her lifeless orbs as the black dots continued to look back at him. She had just been there with him. Just minutes ago, she had been in line with him, talking to him.

He could already start to hear the commotion from the crowd, and some that had family members holding their place were already running over. Tim didn't turn to look. He just wanted his Michelle, to have her eyes snap out of their daze and to stare back at him, not through him.

He didn't even notice as the dark shape started to crawl over Michelle and continue towards him.

* * * *

Brett yawned, his eyes moist in the corner as they fought to stay open. His mouth pulled tight, and he could feel the muscles in his neck tense. His whole body was feeling like it wasn't awake, and there wasn't a single part of him that wanted to be there.

He couldn't remember the last time he had woken up that early. Had he ever?

He didn't want to be up that early now. It wasn't even five in the morning yet. It was unnatural, uncalled for to be there, and to make it worse, he had to listen to that man just drone on and on. He was babbling something about lines and flow of traffic.

Brett really didn't care. Like he really wanted to spend his day after thanksgiving listening to some windbag who thought he could just shout out orders and that they were like sheep that would follow.

"Ha," Brett had to fight from laughing out loud. Sheep. That was like the pack forming outside, sheep being lead to the slaughter.

Just yesterday, he had been dragged with his parents to his grandparents. Over the river and through the woods to their cramped little house somewhere lost in the corn fields of Illinois to endure a long day of his uncles screaming children. His parents didn't want to leave until it was well past eight, which meant they hadn't crossed back into Wisconsin until it neared midnight.

Then he had to be there to listening to this man, who on a normal day, he would consider to be a pretty cool boss. However, any man inflicting the early morning torture was no longer considered to be a nice man.

"So Brett, where are you going to be?"

Brett blinked and looked through the blue clad men and women around him to the man standing at the middle; the man who now called him out for not paying attention.

"Um, walking the line?" Brett said, thankful that Sullivan had told him the plans before Thanksgiving.

"Okay, so, grab your jacket and the item tickets and get out there. Remember one ticket per customer and make sure to pitch our services. I don't want any computers going out without any setups. If they get to register and you haven't sold them, you failed."

"Failed! What the hell did he know?" Brett thought to himself. He couldn't remember the last time he had seen the old man on the sales floor.

Brett grabbed his large heavy winter coat that he had sitting on one of the front displays, made a check for the hand warmers he had kept in the left front pocket and started to walk towards the front door. Behind him, he could hear Jim ramble on to the rest of his troops.

"Troops preparing for war, and this were the battlefield," he thought as he reached the large front metal gate. It clattered loudly in the busy morning, and he wanted to cover his ears against the screeching metal sound. Instead he just clinched his teeth until the metal was pulled far enough to the side, and rested there in its guided path.

He stepped over the metal rail that was the guide for the gate and stood just before the large glass double door and looked out into the darkness of the morning. He could have sworn that the street lights had been on when he had pulled in to the parking lot, but now, as he looked out there, it was dark. Almost completely dark, where usually, he could see the cars parked in the lot.

The employees' cars were always parked towards the back, and a stab of concern spawned that he couldn't see his own car.

He reached for the lock and heard the click as it unlatched with a dead thud. Something was growing in stomach, something wasn't right, and he had a feeling starting to twist in his insides. The hairs along his arms started to rise, and a sudden shock of what felt like electricity started to dance in the air.

Maybe it was just his fear?

"What the hell was there to be afraid of? Come on, man, wake yourself up and get out there. What the hell is there to be afraid of?" He knew he was saying it in his mind more to himself to calm his nerves, but there was still that unnerving feeling that there was something there.

There was something out there that there was to be afraid of. Why else wouldn't he just go out there, and starting working up the line of customers. He was one hell of a salesman. He could walk that line and sell warranties to the most cranky of them and that was all commission money coming straight to his pocket. Who said it didn't pay to be sleazy?

He started to pull on the doors, working to pull them apart. They caught at first, and then started to pull apart with ease, and Brett was met with the cold November chill that was feasting its way through the morning. It was hungry, that cold and it wanted to make him apart of it.

A shiver ran through him.

He took a step out into the darkness and was met with cold stiff plastic assaulting his face, and he instantly remembered why he hadn't been able to see the parking lot from inside.

Jim and in infinite genius to protect the bargains, had covered the front door with that damn black plastic so no one could see into the store. Heaven forbid that anyone could see in and see that we only carried maybe two of some ultra-low priced deal. No, let's keep the customers not knowing so they stand in line for three hours and still were not be able to get what they were waiting for.

It was no wonder why all his managers hated the damn holidays. Brett had only been working there for seven months, and he was already starting to hate them. They ruined his Fourth of July, his Labor Day, and every other single holiday since he had made the mistake of starting there.

Brett closed the door behind him and started to beat against the plastic, working his way to find its end.

"Fuck this." He muttered under his breath.

The cold wet plastic seemed to fight against him, the darkness a small maze he was trying to push his way through. He could almost imagine how fish felt when they were trapped in the net. The damn plastic just wouldn't seem to let him go. The wind just seemed to catch it whenever he would try to push it away from himself, and whip it back into him. It was like there were hands reaching through the plastic trying to grab him.

A sudden strong draft finally pushed the plastic away, allowing him to break free. The wind, a slice of cold air that burned his skin rushed at him and the light from the parking lot revealed itself. He felt a brief relieving sensation of being free and inhaled deeply the clean cool air.

Brett had just a second to enjoy being released from the plastic before he realized that it hadn't been the wind that had been pushing it in against him.

* * * *

Cynthia was rushing, nearly running to reach the break room where she could already hear Jim talking about how they were all going to survive the morning. It was his same speech that he gave every year. The one about what everyone was expected to do, and how certain people were sharks walking the line, while others were given directions on how to do the quick pitch on selling at the register.

Jim could sell, she definitely felt that way about him. He had no soul and would sell a warranty to his dying grandmother even if it cost her last dollar she had. He would still make the sale.

Listen to him and a person could make some money in commissions, and that she did.

But she didn't like being late. She was never late. Her damn alarmed clock, why hadn't it gone off. She was never late.

She knew they were already upset with her, she could tell it from the tone of Aaron's voice when he had called wondering where she was. Thank goodness he had called. She never would have made it otherwise.

She eased her way in to the already crowded room, sneaking her way into the back of the crowd. Jim didn't seem to notice, but Aaron did. It was probably for the best though, so that way he knew that she was there, and wouldn't be trying to call her again. She wondered if anyone else had been late.

"Okay, everyone ready? Everyone know what they are supposed to do?" Jim called out to the crowd.

Cynthia looked over to the new guy. His name was Rick, or Randy, something with an "R". Damn she felt sorry for him. This was never what you wanted to do for your first day. Only a sadistic SOB would put a man on his first day against the morning rush.

She looked back to Jim who was walking over with Randy or Rick or whatever his name was, and was starting to lead him out of the room. Cynthia had to step to the side to let them past, and she caught the evil stare that Jim gave her, then he turned his attention back to "R" and they were heading toward the door.

The rest of the half-awake zombies of the morning employees moved to follow, but Cynthia, her pulse racing from having to hurry, had a quicker step to her walk and was able to follow Jim out the door before anyone else started to really move.

They were all making their way from the back break area, Jim in his long quick manager's stride, "R" eager to please on his first day and Cynthia, with her just being her normal chipper self. However, Cynthia slowed as they were making their way to the front door. She slowed, as the hairs on the back of her neck stood and she realized that something just didn't feel right.

The front of the store was dark. Darker than normal, but that was to be expected with the plastic over the front door. Still that wasn't it. There was something else, something that hung in the air. It was like there was a bad smell of meat gone rank, but it was so faint that she could feel it more than smell it. Then there was also that tickle of a sound. There was a thumping, like something dull being repeatedly knocked against glass.

"Holy shit, is that them beating against the glass?" "R" said as him and Jim headed toward the front door.

Jim stopped just before they both reached it.

Cynthia thought she knew why, too. It was the same reason why she slowed. He felt it too, or he heard it. After all, "R" was right. It did sound like the customers outside were hitting against the glass doors. That is, if they were hitting it in slow motion and no energy.

The repetitive pumps did make it sound like there were many of them, and they wanted in.

"It's time," Jim said as he checked his watch.

"Yeah, but time for what?" Cynthia thought as she watch Jim move to unlock and power on the inner doors. It was time for what?

Cynthia could hear as the other employees started to stop and stand at various spots around her. She took a glimpse at them, and she could so see them all as the walking dead as they all looked so tired and half alive.

She turned back from the crowd of employees behind her in time to watch as the inner doors glided loudly open and Jim strutted his way to the outer doors. The inner doors started to squeak back close, the loud high pitch squeal cutting through the mysterious thumping with its own horror movie soundtrack.

Jim an "R" were cut off from the rest of them as they stood enclosed in the vestibule. Each one taking sides as Jim guided "R" in how the front iron gates folded back away into the sides of the door.

Cynthia stopped watching them and looked to the black tarp still hanging outside the doors. She could see different shapes at different points of the black tarp, pushing through and then hitting into the front glass door.

She could hear the loud "clank" as Jim secured the gate on the left side of the door. The pounding on the door intensified. Jim, without waiting for "R" to finish with his side, came rushing back into the front part of the store.

"Where are all my tech guys!" Jim said as he scanned through his sleeping audience. No one responded. Jim turned back around.

"Where were they?" Cynthia had the fleeting thought as she watched Jim unlock the door and "R" flipped the power switch.

As the door slowly squealed open, even louder than the inner door, no one expected what was about to happen. The door didn't make it halfway and Jim was just about to give his morning "get in line" speech to the customers while reaching to pull down the black tarp when all hell broke loose.

A hand reached through the tarp, grabbing Jim's hand just after he grabbed the tarp. He barely had time to call out, "What th-" when the weight shift on the other side from pulling Jim's arm, to pushing it forward. In a rush of flying black darker than the moonless sky, the tarp rushed forward. The first shapes, falling forward caught in it like it was a fishing tarp.

"R," who had just kept himself a little off to the right, just missed being caught by the falling tarp. Not that it helped him much. The mass crowd, still not seen too well in the darkened vestibule from where Cynthia stood, was quickly stumbling over the first wave of the fallen and their hands quickly were grabbing "R". Their grasp ripped and pulled at his clothes as he started to stumble back. He might have made it away from them as well, had he not backed up against the glass stationary part of the gliding front door.

It was then, as "R" was trying to push against glass that would not move that Cynthia saw what was there. At first she could only see all the pairs of hands, and disembodied arms. The hands themselves were mostly all covered in crimson and dripping, but what they belonged to? It was something like out of a horror flick, the ones that her ex-boyfriend, Kenny, used to always try to get her to watch.

Zombies? Zombies!? She could see the disfigured faces, the blank stare, and the stumbling lurches as they made their way forward. She could tell, though she had tried to never watch those films as there was too much of people getting torn apart, their intestines strewn around like bloody Christmas lights.

She had a passing reminder of having to help her mom put up Christmas lights tomorrow as she started to back up. The zombies had already reached "R" and were starting to pull him apart. They were tearing off limbs, but they were eating into him, pulling his flesh away in large strips. He was screaming in ways that Cynthia didn't know a man could. The loud sound, not sounding like it came from human vocal cords. Then the scream seemed to fill with liquid, gurgling before it was cut off.

Cynthia hadn't stayed around long enough to find out what caused the scream to quit. She had turned tail and run, and she hadn't even waited to see if anyone was following. She cared about them, many of them were her friends, but right now it was survival. She was a four foot petite eighteen year old girl, nothing but a snack to those things. She didn't plan to have herself become an easy snack.

She made it to the back of the center row when she stopped running. She was panting a little, but nowhere near yet worked up. No. Those weekly workouts she had with that hot instructor that she had been continuing to flirt with had kept her in shape.

Behind her she could hear others coming her way, running. The breath caught in her throat as she turned to see who was coming. She kept her body turned, ready to run. All her senses were alive and she felt like she was a deer who had just heard the snap of a twig.

With her head turned back, she saw shapes running towards her. Shadows dancing in the dark, nothing more than outlines running away from the lights surrounding the front.

Cynthia felt her breath catch and her chest seized. The shapes were running and images of running zombies flashed through her head. She tried to think of where to go and where to hide. Where could she go?

"Go! Go go go go GO!" the larger shape yelled. Cynthia recognized his voice. Ryan was yelling at her, and she turned back to run as they neared reaching her.

"Come on! Receiving!" Ryan yelled at her, waving his arm for her to follow. She did quickly. She wasn't sure how many or if anyone else was following. Sure, she hoped there was, but she could only afford to think about herself and get herself safe.

Cynthia heard a loud scream behind her. It wasn't all the way to the front so the Zombies must have been getting closer. She wanted to turn and look to see how far away they were, but no, it wasn't safe.

Ahead, Cynthia could see the light disappear where the sales floor ended and the receiving department began. Her pace faltered as she could imagine once crossing that threshold, it was going to be harder to see what was around the corner. It was too dark in there; they shouldn't be going in. Just what the hell was Ryan thinking?

"Ryan! Wait"

Ryan didn't wait. He kept running and when he reached the corner to turn into receiving, he disappeared into the darkness.

Cynthia didn't linger any longer. She pushed herself harder to catch back up with them, still not sure who the second running figure was. She assumed it was Tommy. The figure was about his size and she couldn't imagine Ryan being there without his twin.

The shadows kept bouncing around her, and she felt like she had entered into one of those fun houses that tried to scare her. She entered into the darkness and all sight was lost. The world around her felt like it was gone and the night was taking over. Like it was its own essence, it was enveloping around her and she was losing herself into some bad horror film. It was the one where everything was coming after her, everything from her nightmares.

Ryan yelled back to her, telling her to hurry. As her eyes adjusted to the little light, she could see him starting to climb his way up the roof access stairs. His boots echoing off the metal stairs as he climbed, she worried that they would be heard if any of those things were nearby.

Tommy was right behind Ryan, and she hurried over to follow them.

"Come on!" he yelled to her, urging her on.

She started to climb, looking up to Ryan as she did so. He was getting near to roof access door. She was afraid they might freeze to death once they got out there, but for the time being, she just wanted to get somewhere safe. Being on a roof where none of those things could get to her was at least one step in the right direction.

Ryan reached the top of the ladder and started to push on the door. She could hear him grunting and then a frustrated cry out.

"Shit! It's locked!"

She kept climbing, though she already feared that they were going to be stuck there.

She heard another kind of grunt. It was one that she had already learned and dreaded recognizing.

The lights of the store turned on. The automatic timer must have finally recognized that it was time to open the store.

Cynthia could see as the first wave of zombies made their way around the corner. They moved slowly. Some of them limping, those it looked like because part of their legs had been eaten through. Most of them just stumbled, walking slowly like they didn't remember how. It was like they were mindless to the point of not knowing who or what they used to be, but that they were moving with a purpose and a desire to do something. Like they wanted something, but didn't know what it was that they wanted?

A sick part of Cynthia that she never knew existed until that very moment said to her, "What separated these shoppers from any of their other customers?" She suppressed the small insane laughter that had been building. The answer wasn't all that funny after all. These shoppers wanted her flesh.

"What are we going to do?" Ryan asked. Cynthia looked back up to him. She was glad to see that she was right, and that it was Tommy there with him. She always liked it when she was right. She just smiled at herself and to them.

She was beginning to realize that she was about to die. It was strange, knowing that it was about to happen, but she was done fighting it. She looked around her. There was no place to go. The large receiving bay doors already had pounding from the other side and the familiar grunts from more zombies. So they were trapped. The only way out was up, and with the freezing cold, even that would have been a death sentence.

She watched as the zombies started to gather below her feet. They were far enough below her, that as they reached up to try and pull her back down, she was still safe.

Above her, Ryan and Tommy were working together to try and break the door open. She just watched them for a brief time. The fear that had her previously gripped her, seemed to have left her as now a strange calm seemed to have washed over her.

She felt her hand release on the cool metal, and she could feel herself falling back. Then the hands, there were many of them, and they all started to tear into her. They grabbed and they clawed, and while she could hear herself screaming she knew that her body was filled with the pain of being ripped apart. She also didn't feel it. Like her mind was already away from it all.

And then everything she had known before was gone. She was gone, and just becoming another one of the many. One of the many cravers, mindlessly craving what they don't even know what they are craving for. She was lost to become a part of the mass.

Short-term recollections of a life, before the ice...
by Sergio Palumbo

The death of a loved one is never an easy event to bear, but there is something worse than that: it is your own death, especially if diagnosed before its time, unexpectedly and predicted on a usual day by a doctor you completely trust. With his fiancé gone, the fair-haired, former middle-aged salesman Frank Herslow could no longer tolerate staying in his house, the same where he had grown up and then had chosen to stay and live for the rest of his life. There were far too many remnants of hopes and projects that would never come true. Unfortunately, the passing of time seemed only to say that death would be coming for him next...

"What went wrong?" he kept asking himself. The doctors had never assured him that his partner would make it, but he had hoped he would, in his heart, anyway.

Although he never drank too much when he lived with his woman, now dead, Frank soon discovered that alcohol seemed to have a beneficial effect on his mind. But it made his body's condition even worse, and it took all the drinks he could handle to make him temporarily forget about the life that had been so cruelly taken away from him. Still, he could not stay drunk forever, of course. At first he didn't want to follow his old doctor's instructions: he didn't feel good, but there were too many thoughts and worries by then.

"I can well understand why you're acting this way," said the man in charge of his case at his hometown hospital. Frank knew the doctor well, and he had been told by his physician: "I'm sure you'd prefer to forget your bad health, at present, but you mustn't act this way. Just hear me out..."

And so the doctor had convinced him, eventually. That was why Frank had followed his doctor's suggestion, undergoing a peculiar, new treatment that another medical facility was experimenting with. Their goal was to improve the procedure that year in order to save people affected by particular fatal illnesses - the same situation the man was in.

He didn't have the funds to pay such an expensive procedure, but his doctor told him that the facility was willing to wave the fee, because they were looking for people who were eager to attend their new healing programs. The participants in the study would need to be tested daily, requiring thorough checks involving a series of experimental steps.

The facility to which the doctor referred was the newly completed **Up Forward Medical Center**, located in the hills north of the town of Waterbury, Vermont. The location looked massive and followed modern trends of architecture of tall buildings in the medical field. The area was designed for the site to have a lot of light and ventilation. Also, on the outside, there were elaborate gardens. He was going to get used to that place from then on out, but he didn't that yet.

"It's a miracle you have managed to survive as long as you have..." These were the words the skinny, short-haired chief physician of the medical facility -- an Haitian individual of the apparent age of 40, wearing an expensive brownish suit-- told him

144

the first day he entered his office. After a complete exam, the doctor added "If you had waited a few days more, there would have been nothing we to do for you."

"I didn't think my condition was that bad already," Frank had replied. He was really worried now, tearing his untidy hair out, while thinking about his whitish skin which looked more and more tired each day, as a matter of fact. Both of those symptoms were signs of the increasing illness that he had tried to ignore so far.

"Unfortunately, bad health tends to worsen with the passing of the time, it doesn't get better by itself, without help or treatment from anybody, you know." Both dark eyes of the physician stared at him for a while.

The man made no reply.

"There are a few tiresome forms to be filled out." And that being said, the slim Haitian handed an embarrassed Frank some papers, eventually.

On the night of his arrival, the newly accepted patient received a bath, a very good meal and a clean bed. The room was pleasant and endowed with all the new products that up-to-date technology could provide in the TV and sound system field. There was also a wide window that allowed a pleasant view of the gardens outside.

The next morning the treatment began.

"You won't be getting any alcohol to drink here," the chief physician stated clearly from the beginning. This had showed Frank that the clinic was well aware of his condition and wouldn't allow any breaking of the rules, now that he had been accepted into the study, under fear of being dropped from the program. "Not one drop. If you're thirsty, you can have a glass of water or juice whenever you need it, of course."

At first he had believed that water couldn't satisfy his desires. In fact, the first day he started to experience the symptoms of withdrawal, both physical and emotional, but the medications the doctors gave him proved to be effective and soon he felt much better. That night he never shook, he slept well, and he almost forgot his desire for his usual liquors. The personnel working there appeared to be very capable and knew what to do in order to help him, as a matter of fact.

That night he lay in his bed, staring at the moon and stars outside his window. Frank didn't know yet that this was going to become one of the last times he would look at those lights with his own eyes, in full consciousness and presence of mind. Actually, the moon and the many stars would always be there and look the same, but soon he would be different, not the man he was before. Not even human, in a way… How could he have ever visualized that, after all? Surely, he couldn't even imagine such a thing that night.

* * * *

Since the beginning of civilization, people have used stone and metals found on or close to the Earth's surface to build their houses with, creating impressive buildings and starting new business and activities everywhere. Many different minerals were used to make early tools and weapons. But with the passing of the centuries, mankind had developed more and more specialized ways of mining to get to the valuable ore fields and even further to the deepest underground. This development had also happened in the far recesses of the world, in some icy and deserted areas, especially in modern times.

Named after a man who was the Prime Minister of Canada from 1911 to 1920, **Borden Island** was known as the 172nd largest island in the world, with only two types of terrain: a gravel-strewn landscape on the northern side and a region of darker, more elevated ground in the south, where the maximum height did not exceed 491 feet. Unusual for arctic islands, there were no lakes on it. Laying north of Mackenzie King Island, in the Queen Elizabeth Islands, it was property of both the Northwest Territories (its larger portion, actually) and Nunavut. Having an area of 1,079 square miles in size, 58.3 miles long and 51 miles wide, it had been previously reported in history as a single landmass by Vilhjalmur Stefansson who made the first known sighting of the island in 1916. But in 1947, during an aerial survey by the Royal Canadian Air Force, the place was found to be two islands divided by the Wilkins Strait.

Winters were long and difficult there. With daytime highs around minus 4 degrees F, and lows around −40 degrees F, summers were short and very cool, as well. No trees stood on the island, anywhere. No one lived there in 2052 as a matter of fact, as the zone was not inhabited by stable settlers nor had any currently recognized outpost where citizens usually lived. After all, the **Northwest Territories** only had an overall population of 43,462 at that time, spread out across a very wide country. It wasn't strange that there were no inhabitants on that island so far away - apart from some researchers who very rarely went there for scientific purposes. It was covered with ice and had a really unpleasant climate. But it was because of one of those surveys, or better, as a result of some discoveries that were made on it, that everything changed in 2053…and the destiny and the importance of the island itself became something very different, in the end.

When the first employees of the **Outwards Science and Technology Modern Company**, also known simply as **OSTMC**, came to the island and set up the first camp on its eastern coast, they found something very unexpected. Their surprise at what they found, could all be explained by the many failures in satellite detections that had resulted during the previous months because of some unprecedented signal disturbances. These had occurred when satellites in Earth's orbit tried to investigate the subterranean geology of the island, in order to ascertain if there were valuable minerals there that looked rare and precious enough to be worth excavating. Of course, any company that found a rich deposit had the right to control and manage it as it wished. So, the researchers soon understood that there was a lot of work to be done over the course of the next months, indeed.

With a generally low shoreline, cut by several streambeds, the only landforms on the island were some low hills in the southeast, while its northwest coast fronted on the Arctic Ocean. This was not an easy location to set a mining facility, certainly. Besides the terrible temperatures, the windy weather, and the difficult ground that always remained frozen and almost impenetrable, there was something else which made all that even worse and almost impossible: the origin of the signal disturbances. This was the source of the problem that made everything so difficult, it was the heart of the reason why they had come here to begin with, spending so much and investing so many resources.

Getting to what was in the ground proved even tougher than ever imagined. The only thing their labor and machines were able to do was just remove the ice from the surface, but nothing else... The ramp road constructed three years before showed signs of approximately 12,20 inches of upwards movement between June and August every year, because of the summer season's partial melting and usual movements. It appeared from the way the edge of an ice sheet looked, depended upon the balance between ablation and the amount of ice arriving from the accumulation area: if the velocity of the ice didn't increase quickly from the bottom up -- and each successive elementary flow layer produce enough ice to balance ablation -- an excess of icy amount delivered to the margin would form an ice cliff. Anyway, silt and rock bands where most of the inclusions were in contact with each other deformed less readily than the surrounding ice. The whole area was mainly a plain, a snowy and empty surface, with some accumulation of round boulders, apparently flattened at the top. Their most characteristic feature was the presence of glacial striations on the flat top surface. This was considered good evidence of ice continuously sliding over the ground.

To gain access to the very rare mineralized package within such an area -- obtained through a Mining Rights Lease -- it was necessary to mine through a lot of waste material which was not of interest to the **OSTMC** company. As was commonly the case, more waste than ore was mined during the course of the life of an excavation site. The waste removal and placement was a major cost to mining operators and to facilitate detailed planning, the precise geological and mineralization characterization of the waste material formed an essential part of the exploration program.

In such difficult zones underground mining, which was already very expensive and demanding, was done only when the rocks, minerals, or gemstones were too far underground to get out with surface mining. On this island, far away from the rest of the mainland, excavations probably would have never occurred unless some very precious substances or resources were found. Minerals like gold perhaps or, in their case, the very valuable and most rare: **Icelandite**, which could be found nowhere else on Earth – except in eight small rocks that had been extracted years before in Iceland, from whence the name originated. Later it had been detected on some asteroids in space, not yet reachable by Mankind, as some launched probes had revealed in a few reports over the course of the last years.

Unfortunately, it was impossible for this mineral to be produced through some innovative process, or to be created artificially in a laboratory or factory. There were already many mines in the Northwest Territories, like the famous Diavik Diamond Mine in the North Slave Region, the Pine Point Mine (zinc) and the Con Mine (gold) which had just been reactivated recently, along with dozens of others - but none of them could be really reputed as important as this one on Borden Island or as incredibly valuable.

In order for the minerals to be taken out of the mine, the mining-machines had to make underground rooms to work in. The companies usually chose the best way to get the minerals out. Most excavation was done using "continuous mining" that put into action several types of modern semi-automated or robotic machines to cut sliced layers from the walls. This process was useful when mining involved diamonds, copper or gold minerals. For example, such a thing usually meant that there was less drilling and put less workers down in the mines. All that was much safer than the old kind of mining. But here things looked really different.

The waste coming out of a common ore mine was usually classified as either sterile or mineralized (with a potential for problems) and the movement and stacking (or dumping) of this material formed a major part of the mine planning. In addition, the waste dump designs had to meet all the regulatory requirements of the country in whose jurisdiction the mine was located. It was also common practice for the companies to do the rehabilitation of the dumps to an international acceptable standard, which in some cases meant that higher standards than the local regulatory standard were applied.

On the contrary, what came out of the underground here was **deadly**: no human workers could operate next to the mines, nor in the vicinity on the surface. And deadly meant, in this case, that the machines' electronic instruments and delicate devices were heavily damaged because of the radioactive substances coming out of the mine - so much so that they were soon broken beyond repair.

After the first long and unexpected stops, the company employees knew that if mining did not resume immediately, it would be very difficult to keep the plant running. OSTMC had tried unsuccessfully to change the instruments frequently and reinforce their casings, but failures had become a daily business.

Eventually the month came when it had finally ceased to have recourse to even to those procedures. Afterwards, another perfect alternative had been discovered, unexpectedly, thanks to one of the several medical laboratories that were managed by some of the many subsidiaries of their company worldwide…**human workers that were not humans**, at least not anymore.

Some government departments of the Northwest Territories -- like the ones of Education and Employment, Health and Social Services, Industry and even the Department of Justice -- would have shown great interest in their company's real activity up there - if they had ever discovered the truth, certainly. But they simply couldn't even imagine what was really going on in there, so far away from every inhabited town or country.

The first miners the company used died in a matter of days because of the radioactive properties of the valuable minerals taken from the mine. Their administrative offices and the company doctors made their best efforts to cover it up and they were able to keep the accidents and all the casualties hidden.

Julius de Chacon, the attractive, forty-seven-year-old CEO of OSTMC knew he couldn't maintain an ongoing silence about the many deaths that would happen if vulnerable humans kept working in such areas. Even though OSTMC only used people with no relatives, or men whose sons and parents would never care or think about their beloved, too many dead men or disappearances would arouse suspicions, and start inquiries by local policemen (the few their company couldn't bribe in the end…). Investigations by government authorities back on the mainland were also possible.

So the only choice was to make use of a different kind of laborer. Expendable workers, as a matter of fact…Zombies were the only answer to that, be it bizarre or simply hard to believe!

'We dare to do what nobody else would…' the man thought, putting up his black hair and looking amusedly at the snowy, freezing scenery that lay outside of the window. He was in the middle of four reinforced walls that made up the room he stayed in. 'Profit doesn't come from nothing, there is hard work to be done here, and only tough, indestructible guys can do it...'

It had been a long, freezing winter - at least according to what he had been told by the few technicians who always stayed at the facility. They lived far away from the deadly mining site and had said this to him when he arrived yesterday. Summer didn't seem to be too much milder, but thankfully the sky finally looked clear at present, even though a very bad weather system had tormented the area that morning.

Within two hours, hopefully, the guests the CEO was waiting for would arrive, at last.

* * * *

At times Frank felt some parts of his body aching or he suffered because of a stiffened gait. At times he even fell into a state of unconsciousness. But the doctors reassured him, making it clear that it was all due to the process he was slowly undergoing during those initial days in their facility. After all, he should have been glad he didn't feel the need to drink anymore or the deep pain he had in his chest when he just had first arrived there.

For most of that first morning, he had been attached to a tiny plastic tube put into his upper arm. Infusions usually lasted from 30 minutes to a few hours, but that time it seemed to take longer than usual. A mixed drug solution flowed from a plastic container through the tubing, controlled by a machine's electronic pump. The doctor decided the overall length of that procedure on a day-by-day basis. The morning before, he had had another drug put into his spinal column, in addition, by means of a small device going into it directly, and that device had to stay in place under his skin until the treatment was finished. On another day, instead of that, the substances had been given to him by way of his abdominal cavity.

Such sessions didn't hurt even though Frank felt the brief discomfort of all that, undoubtedly. But it was for a greater good, as the doctors kept telling him, after all.

Although exhausted, he was unable to sleep easily that night. For the first time in a long while, he thought again about his lost love. The hours slowly ticked slowly by. Around early morning the night nurse came to the door, entered the patient's room and gave him some pills.

"Some other colorful medicines for me, instead of breakfast today?" he asked. The nurse, with a round face and rich lips, her long blonde hair hanging down, didn't respond and simply smiled in return, handing the man a glass of water. He swallowed all the pills he had been handed, then a sort of unconsciousness seemed to wrap around his mind, getting a strong hold on him, like the grip of a giant on a dwarf.

Strange sensations filled his thoughts, making him disturbed and stressed. At a certain point he even seemed to be in a wide expanse, shadowed in darkness, with a strong light coming from above, where cries and yells could be heard everywhere. Somebody was working on his body, or so he imagined, and some dead tissues and bloody organs were being taken out of his chest and put in the trash, as if they were things he just didn't need anymore. But he wasn't able to move or oppose all that - or even speak to the dim figures he saw around, busy attending their unknown job in that unrecognized location. It was a very long, uneasy sleep.

The next morning, when the same nurse came in with the same pills for him, the man asked if, by chance, he had undergone some operation that night, maybe because of some unexpected emergency or heart failure.

"People who are in withdrawal often see things that aren't really there. If you didn't rest well last night, just close your eyes and try to get some sleep now."

But when the light of dawn filled his window, the man was still awake. Unconsciousness came again, however, just a few moments later.

* * * *

The AS 370BA, 'Squirrel B' single-engine helicopter flew over a seemingly limitless white surface that the pilot and passengers were finally able to see. The previously overcast sky had been blocking the view for most of the trip. The rotorcraft was capable of transporting up to 7 people, other than the two crewmembers, and was able to fly up to 700 miles. It was mainly used for ice reconnaissance missions or to assist ship navigation through the icy expanse all year long. But this wasn't the case today, indeed.

Arctic helicopter operations were not radically different from well-established flights in far-north lands, but there were many things to be prepared in advance. Properly maintaining the helicopter in order to have the engine function adequately in such a difficult environment was a top priority certainly, as the locations to be reached usually were far away from parts and backup services. Of course, some pilots with a long and varied experience -- which was not easy to develop -- were always needed for those insidious flights. Such crafts provided the only link between the mainland and Borden Island, so far, except for some vessels that were privately owned by OSTMC. A few of these regularly made the route to the only facility the company had built there.

Everything they were able to see now was very different from the few satellite images they had been shown before. These were shown in an unusual and secret way, along with the convocation for that meeting on such a lonely island far away from all the other places they had visited before. It didn't seem possible to always get data from the usual sources about that location -- only a few of the passengers had ever heard anything about the island until the day before they had been called -- and this fact was another strange thing about that long trip of theirs.

Low, north-facing escarpments lined the south coast, as far as they were able to see from their seats, while a long field-of-ice drained from the east and then braided together as they neared the coastline.

Just down there the OSTMC facility -- kept in solitude on purpose and built on that site, unbeknown to most of mankind -- finally appeared on the plain expanse. And then the orange rotorcraft landed.

* * * *

The following day Frank walked through the halls of the medical facility, arriving at the gardens like an individual in a daydream, his tired eyes attesting to his lack of sleep.

The three different medical sessions of the long treatment he had been given the evening before had proved more painful than ever. The infusions put into his body had lasted for two hours and had left him with a strange sensation in his head.

When the man sat at the table for his lunch, he wasn't even able to eat. Then he remained out there for a while, unable to walk away or ask for someone who could help him. Nobody around noticed his silent cry for a nurse, nor his absent-minded look.

A doctor came to his table later on, and touched his wrist, then examined his complexion, which seemed to be very pale that morning, and simply opened his mouth in a sort of wide smile, or so it looked to him.

"Now, here we are, finally…" the Haitian chief of the structure said, as he got to where Frank was, probably called by some of his nurses.

* * * *

"Good day," said Julius de Chacon, the middle-aged CEO of OSTMC. He was wearing a clear blue arctic jacket, and pleasantly greeted the group of five men and two women who had been waiting to meet him since that morning at the facility office of the company on Borden Island. The bad weather that week had delayed their helicopter which had some difficulties at getting to the base on time. In fact they had landed just ten minutes ago, at 2:00 PM.

The guests, all dressed in heavy clothes mainly in red and orange, with expensive gloves and huge hoods that reflected their tastes for the most pricey winter sports attire, were led into a wide room all painted in green. From there the CEO himself led them along a seemingly unending covered path directly connecting that part of the facility -- built next to the heliport on the icy surface of that side of the island -- to the main buildings of the snow-proof structure itself. The walk made them all look about carefully, amazed at the notable job that had been done throughout the entire way in order to create such a perfect passage, well protected from the windy gusts coming from the outside.

The CEO noticed the stupor and admiration in his guests' eyes and pointed out: "This is all due to the hard labor of our workers whom you will soon meet, my dear chairmen. We can continue this way, please." And that being said, he turned to the right, advancing along another covered path that looked separated from the one they were walking a minute before by means of a squared junction made up of a soft, hi-tech matter.

By placing his mouth near to the communicator on the wall, the CEO simply said, "Bring in Subject One". A few moments later the two heavy doors at the end of the room opened wide and a slim technician came in. He was next to an individual, pale of skin on a slender body dressed in a white robe, not taller than an ordinary man, a wide collar around his neck, who was coming nearer in a sort of mechanized gait. His arms were perfectly moving forwards and inwards like a well-trained and undoubtedly disciplined soldier, actually.

The hairless technician with an amusedly pointed nose seemed to lead the strange man to a sort of operating table, turned up, where he was placed briefly before being attached to some strings connected to his shoulders. This left him dangling just a few inches off the floor.

The life in the eyes of the one being examined seemed to be absent, an expressionless look on his face, no sign of rebellion or doubt on his quiet features. You could say it was one of those dummies you would see inside some shop window, except that he was alive and he looked like a real man, even though a bit weird and different from a common individual, of course.

* * * *

As soon as Frank woke up, he just found himself in the same room where he met the Haitian chief physician the day he had first entered that medical facility. He was able to easily recognize all the furnishings and the desk in front of him, also the window looked familiar to him.

"We've almost reached our goal, my dear patient..." the skinny doctor who sat at the other side of the room told him. "You're almost dead..."

With a coarse voice, as he didn't appear to be capable of speaking in his usual tone, the man replied "So...your treatment...was...unsuccessful..."

"**On the contrary**, it went perfectly!" the other stated. "It has proven to be a long process by which we have killed off your tissues and many organs one at a time. During the several treatments you had, we were able to keep the rest of your body temporarily alive by making it adapt to the loss of some functions as it was dying little by little, until we could arrive at the next step, in order to keep it in a good overall state. Now you're exactly the way we wanted you to be."

"Did you…want…me died?" Frank said, with many difficulties in expressing clearly his words.

The Haitian man simply nodded slowly.

"So, why have… you been treating…me?"

"Your condition was not good at the beginning, because of your terminal illness, which was made even worse by your drinking problem. You needed to be in good health again at the start of the zombification process. There was no other way if we wanted to finally succeed at making **a good zombie out of you…!**"

These were the last words Frank heard and understood just before losing control of his own mind forever and becoming an absent-minded slave, a person bereft of consciousness and self-awareness, a sort of thing that was alive no more.

The doctor, in his expensive suit, looked at Frank's face with a vivid amusement in his eyes. The job seemed to have been a success. After all, according to the mission of their laboratories, as indicated in their statement, they did buy cadavers for science and research purposes only, from time to time.

But that was not exclusively true. Actually, they turned living people into corpses. And then into useful zombies, untiring zombie-laborers, as a matter of fact.

* * * *

"Ladies and gentlemen," announced Luis, "here is a fine example of one of our best products, the one that makes this entire mining camp function well." Luis then addressed the small group of businessmen and businesswomen next to him and added, "He is one of the zombies we have at work in this facility. They are dead beings yet able to walk around and to respond to the orders they are given via radio collars applied directly to their neck. This is exactly the same as computers responding to a selected program. You could think of them as animated corpses brought back to a peculiar life by means of our medical procedures, mixing experimental science with magical energy - that our doctors from the island of Haiti have been able to test, improve and bring to perfection in our few laboratories spread here and there worldwide."

"A very notable example of science put to good work!" exclaimed one of the businessmen named Gogean, who was of Rumanian descent. He was a graying man of about forty, even though his mouth and his overall appearance showed that - in reality - he was much older. His youthful appearance was likely the result of some "re-youth-ing" procedure that was very trendy nowadays, and followed especially by the wealthy, over-sixty crowd.

There was a brief silence showing awe and interest among the guests inside the conference room.

"In Africa, whence this ancient practice came and where was first developed, such doctors were called bokors, but in Haiti they have other names. If you just put aside the legends and terrible tales for frightening children you maybe have already heard about, the fact is that our valuable specialists make use of powerful active drugs taken from Haitian Voodoo and modified according to the most recent finds and studies in the field. There are still many medical secrets to be discovered about this branch of science, certainly, secrets that are now completely unknown, but our researchers are still working on those."

"Impressive!" shouted a dark-haired seventy-year-old woman from South America called Encarna, who had the face of a thirty-year-old girl. "He seems to be alive but he doesn't look like a living being."

"Thank you for your comment…" the CEO replied. "Now just let me explain something about the way we can get this result, apart from the secret parts of the procedure that we aren't allowed to tell you, of course…"

Everyone else in the room smirked amusedly, except the technician next to the zombie who looked like a sort of robot. In a way, you could even consider him a sort of zombie, too, if he hadn't had acne on his naturally pink complexion and a few sweat drops on his very hairy eyebrows, actually.

"In the past some living persons were said to be turned into zombies, due to the fabled bokor of the old times, just by special powders introduced into the blood stream (usually via a wound or a medical procedure). The truth is that a very important powder in this process was mainly tetrodotoxin, a powerful neurotoxin found in some fish of the Tetraodontidae, along with another dissociative drugs known as datura. By creating a death-like state, the will of the victims would be entirely subjected to that of the bokors themselves only after re-awakening into an absent-minded state. Since the past, in the Haitian society, such individuals who underwent a similar process were said to roam around the graves, exhibiting an unconscious persona usually, a sight that made people horrified and scared cause of all that, you know."

Julius paused for a moment, staring into everyone's eyes before continuing.

"Thanks to this new medical treatment of ours, the procedure could be thought of as an ongoing cycle of birth, death and rebirth – at least into a zombie condition, anyway." He almost sneered at this last phrase of his, clearly amused for the funny quote, in a way.

Everybody else in the room smiled broadly in return. The chairmen of the subsidiaries of **OSTMC** acclaimed their guest CEO, making it obvious that they all deeply loved their higher ranking officer. Or so it had to appear, of course. There was only one problem: they were many and there was only one of him. This gave birth to a fierce rivalry among the representatives of the other branches of OSTMC, in order to appear like the most up-and-coming professional or the best person whom the CEO himself had to rely on for the future steps of their company.

"He seems so mild-mannered, so apparently stunned," said Eufemia, a businesswoman in the group. She had exceedingly beautiful features with long, unnatural and wondrous chestnut/blonde/black hair, not a result of some dyeing but achieved only through weeks of many skin transplants from several donors' heads. These transplants usually came from poor and needy yet beautiful young girls whose photos were chosen from the databank of the company working in the field.

"Between ten hours of hard work under extreme circumstances and low temperatures, sometime the units experience a sort of pause, as if the neuronal paths, which have been modified as a consequence of our secret medical process, need to recharge for a while, maybe…it is not yet perfectly explained, indeed…"

"Do they ever dream?" another person asked.

"Actually, such subjects never go really to sleep, even for a nap, but the cerebral graphs we took and checked from time to time showed that maybe, at times, they have glimpses of their past lives, the ones they had when they were still humans, of course."

"Could this interfere with their activity anytime?" a bearded, short man asked, as if he was a bit worried.

"Not at all. They just forget everything as soon as they begin to work again. These are not zombies as you have maybe seen in movies or in some stories, they are a product of modern science, through programs that the common world doesn't know of yet, even though it indirectly benefits greatly from all of them."

"So, they're the perfect laborers, with no interference coming from the trade unions, anyway…"

"They are submissive and obedient and immediately do as they are told, by using the proper signal or the right command via the radio collar at their neck, of course," the higher-ranking officer went on.

"What if," another chairman finally dared to say, "…what if one of those would escape from the grip of your technicians and get to a public space, be it in town or elsewhere?"

The CEO's blue pupils hardened, "You make an interesting point, my good man. Actually, there's no danger about that, as the radio collar is set so that it can always control the one connected to it. Beyond that, just in case some unpredictable, very bad occurrence would happen and we'd lose control of it, the device is designed to release a destructive acid inside the body of the worker and have the corpse dissolved in a matter of minutes.

"The peculiar substance is activated whenever the radio collar doesn't receive a specific input from our main headquarters which uses a satellite communication system to stop the signal emission on time every single hour. So you can say that's enough of a precaution for that, can't you? We surely don't want strange, dead men walking around in town with a zombie-like appearance, or zombies lurking around the woods out back, you know. People would be asking who they are and might start many investigations about them."

The person who had received the answer nodded openly, glad for the convincing explanation he had been given.

Eufemia asked the man. "Do you think that the first thirty units will be available on time, so they can begin working soon at our new mining camp in the Yemen desert?"

"I can assure you that everything will be delivered according to our contract. As a matter of fact - that zombie standing before you now will be part of the first group of your new, untiring laborers."

There was suddenly a continuous beeping sound. Lucius reached into his pocket, looked at the display on his tripad and saw that he had very little time left. "Unfortunately other important appointments and office duties call me away. Now if you want to walk this way for lunch, even if it's a bit late, we'll be serving a lovely meal soon." The others did as ordered, quietly.

While going away from the laboratory, the CEO seemed to be a bit pensive. Just by looking one more time at the subject dangling from the machinery he had been attached to for that brief demonstration, he thought that this zombie had been the first of a long series in their project, a daring new line of business which had proved profitable, in the end. His technicians called it Frank, but the name was not important, of course.

As a matter of fact, he almost disliked to deprive such a facility of that zombie, as he still reminded himself of the hard labor Frank had done: digging for several weeks, through many yards of frozen, difficult ground without stopping. He had moved so many rocks and so much snow, night and day, all alone, before other zombies had reached this location over many months -- as their treatment was going on -- and had now formed a group of more than 100 untiring workers so far...

At that point, as the CEO thought of the Coat of Arms of the Northwest Territories that consisted of two gold fish guarding a rose, symbolic of the magnetic North Pole. He smirked and thought that it would be appropriate if there was also a stylized zombie-like figure depicted there, given the notable amount of riches this new kind of persistent laborer excavated out of the natural resources of that country, for so many months.

It was really a pity to lose that one, who would now be placed at work in the new camp under the hot desert Sun in

Ramlat al-Sab`atayn in north-central Yemen, very far away from that frozen island. But maybe that would also be a nice change for him and the other twenty-nine units: a varied setting in which to work, turning from an icy climate and scene to a new one, composed of sunlight all day long far, far away. Which would have been impossible temperatures for common men, a sort of hell underground.

That project promised to be very rich in opportunities and profits, but such a demanding activity couldn't be done by usual employees, because of the very high temperatures and all the rest involved, of course. Not to speak of the very expensive wages regular human laborers had demanded in order to work down there, wearing costly environmental suits!

Surely the CEO didn't even think there was something immoral going on about all that. He simply shrugged his shoulders. After all, as he used to say, 'business is business…'

Survival
by Jason R. Davis

Winona tried to analyze what she had seen. She needed to figure it out. She was a nurse, a medic, and was used to saving people's lives. It was what she did. It was what she was trained to do. Sure, she had other military training and other talents, but it was her calling to help others.

When she had seen the first attack, she had hurried away from it. She had made her way down the aisle, only thinking of herself and how she had to get out of there. She wasn't sure what had been going on, but she had seen people killed. Her first instinct when not in uniform had kicked in, and she had rushed away.

She had made it to the back, past where the customers were supposed to be, and into the stockroom. There wasn't much there, but she saw two fire doors and the loading dock. She could make it out the fire doors. She figured it would probably set off some type of alarm, but she would be gone. She would be safe, away from the carnage that was happening at the front of the store. That was, of course, unless there were more people out back. No, that didn't make any sense. What was going on up front was a cluster fuck and not a planned killing spree. She at least knew that, but that didn't matter. All that mattered to her right now was the door.

She ran to the fire door and pushed into it. The metal on metal of the latch release clanged loudly in the open area. She was almost out of there; she could almost feel the warm air and hot sun hitting her face.

In her mind's eye, she saw the open field that lay beyond the door. Of course, in reality, there was an alley, loading dock, and then houses, but in her mind she saw that field. Daisy's blossomed, and there was clear blue sky, as she burst out, running to some kind of freedom. She wouldn't have to think about the death, blood, or body parts that she had seen at the front of the store because she would be away from it all, smelling freshly cut grass, flowers, and the calm breeze of the ocean.

She stopped before the emergency alarm on the door went off, and let her head rest against the cool metal. She couldn't leave. Not yet. She would never be able to make it to that freedom. Not when she didn't know if those people were okay. There had been people still alive up there, people that she had left to die. That wasn't her. It wasn't like her to leave people behind. Not only was it her duty, her obligation to take care of people and help them, but that person she enjoyed and loved being would never be able to live with herself if she left. How would she be able to look back on this day years from now if she knew that there might be people alive who will die if she didn't help them?

She kicked the lock on the receiving doors, and looked wistfully at the fire door. The back area she had gone into wasn't separated by a door. In fact, all she had done was gone to the back of the store. There was a cement wall that kept customers from seeing back there, but there was no barrier to keep anyone out. There was a high row of large metal beams in what looked like fixed scaffolding, and mounted on them were large white wire shelves where various items were stored. She had to run around this when she had found the large receiving door. From where she was now, she couldn't see out onto the sales floor.

166

There was a little path where more shelving was stored. It looked like someone had been working back there recently. There was a ladder set up, and the white display shelving used throughout the store was stacked haphazardly about, as though someone had just left it while moving it around. It was in piles for sorting, but it did make it hard for anyone to walk around. It was an excellent place for a person to hide.

She thought momentarily about climbing back there. Maybe she could hide until someone came for her. Maybe help would be there soon, and then everything would be okay. She would be safe; they would all be safe. But if she wasn't going to try and go back to the front and help those people, she might as well have gone out the fire door.

She headed back to where the receiving area ended and the main store began. It was odd with how the store just transitioned back there into the receiving area. It was a wide open space, just going into the back area, but it was still obvious when a person reached the threshold that they were entering a forbidden part of the store. The floor itself turned from overly waxed linoleum to dark gray cement. The lighting, while it was still the same bulbs, seemed to not be as bright, and the air was cooler. It really did almost feel like entering a tomb.

She reached the edge of the threshold and stood near the wall. She just didn't know what she should do, or how she should do it. Where should she start? What she needed was some kind of diversion to get whoever was up at the front of the store away from that area. That was assuming that they were still at the front of the store. They may be searching the aisles, looking for more people. It would be impossible to say how many there were, or where they were right now. And if she did do a diversion, how would it not bring them back to her? Did she have a timer to set something up?

She pulled out her cell phone, and turned it on. It seemed like it took forever for the black screen to light up, the little apple to glow and then fade, and then the blank screen that waited for her to do something. She quickly unlocked it, and felt that sudden pang of desire. She wished she could just call someone and be saved. She guessed she could try to call emergency services again, see if maybe the situation had been resolved. After all, she may be playing hide-and-seek for no reason. The cavalry may already be there and she could just walk up front and report in.

Something crashed from the front of the store. Quickly, she moved to the side, ducking behind the receiving wall. The only way someone could see her once she was crouched down would be for them to be walking into receiving, and even then she was sure that, as long as she didn't move too much, no one would turn to look in her direction.

She looked back at her phone. It stilled showed no signal. A small blip of a bar did form, and she had a glimmer of hope rush through her, but the bar disappeared and the phone again went back to searching. Damn department stores; it always seemed to happen whenever she was shopping. She would always lose signal when she was getting to the back of the store. She should have thought of that.

"Fuck," she whispered to herself. That noise at the front of the store probably meant that it wasn't going to be good up there. She didn't know if anyone had helped any of the victims. When things started happening, she had hurried to the back. There was always the chance that the two violent teenagers could have been subdued by other people. It has been mostly quiet, and she had no way of knowing what was going on until she went up there and checked it out.

But if they weren't subdued, she still had to worry about them. At first she had thought the one with the gun had been trying to help them. The longer she thought about it, she realized that there was no way he could have actually shot the biter. He had to have been faking it. They were doing some kind of weird theatrics, and they had to be working together. She would have to worry about at least two people.

Winona turned and looked towards the front of the store, keeping close to the receiving wall and using it as cover. The store had grown very quiet over the last ten minutes, and it was hard to believe that it was even open. The right side of the store had office items, office furniture in different sets and different office chairs. None of it would allow her any decent cover to hide behind, so she looked to the left. There she saw the high rows of shelving that ran parallel with the main aisle. She could use these. She figured she wanted to flank around, go along the left side, use the shelves for as much cover as she could, and make her way back to the front. She hoped to even make it far enough that she could get a view of the people that had been attacked, and maybe help them.

She still needed a diversion. She looked back at her cell phone, the small print in the corner saying still saying "no service".

Her gut twisted with an idea. It would make noise, but it would work. She was sure of that. It would also leave her without her phone.

She looked over towards the office area. There was a lot of open space. If she was to do it over there, she could easily be seen trying to set it up. While it would be optimal, as it was far on her right flank and would be far from her projected position, setting it up might get her seen. She couldn't risk it.

Unlocking her phone again, she set the alarm clock. She made sure to set multiple alarms because the last thing she wanted was for them to come back there and quickly give up on finding her. Five minutes was more than enough time for her to get to the side wall and work her way up along the flank. She just hoped that it was going to be loud enough for them to hear it.

* * * *

She took a step forward, and was about to step out of the shadows and run to the back shelf. She would be visible from the front of the store for a brief time, and she knew she would have to make a quick dash to keep from being seen.

Her feet nearly slipped out from under her when the loud ringing sounded from overhead. It wasn't an alarm bell. No, she had heard it before in her frequent trips there to shop. It was an incoming phone call that had gone unanswered by the people in the front of the store. If they didn't answer soon enough, the phone call would ring overhead in the PA system. Someone was calling into the store.

Winona had to catch herself to keep from falling. She continued to the center aisles, and stopped when she was at the end of it. The sound of the phone ringing helped hide her running. She felt odd running like that, like she was a child trying to hide from her parents. It just didn't feel real.

She moved to look down the aisle, but still stayed close to the back shelves. She tried to hold onto the shelf, as she leaned forward and looked around it. The store was very still. It didn't feel like the place was even open anymore. There hadn't been a lot of customers before, but now it definitely felt like she was the only one here. She still couldn't see anything down the aisle. Was there anyone even still around? She tried to stay down, as she went the next aisle over. The phone rang again, the sound echoing off the linoleum and seeming to vibrate through her. What the hell was she thinking? Who did she think she was? She wasn't some hero. She helped, yes, but she wasn't Rambo or staring in some Bruce Willis film. What the hell did she think she was doing?

Her job, that's what she was doing. She never should have run to the back. That wasn't her instinct, or it shouldn't have been. Her training was to run to the action, not run away from it. What would her superiors have said if they had seen her running?

170

That's what civilians did, and she had lost that right when she had joined the Guard. She was ashamed of herself. At the time, she had convinced herself that it was because she wasn't in uniform so she had reacted differently. The uniform is a symbol, but that shouldn't matter. Damn, she should still have done her duty.

She looked down the next aisle and still didn't see anyone. She hurried across the opening and stopped. Her lungs burned, and her head swam. Spots danced in the air around her, clouding her vision, and she had closed her eyes to let out a long breath. She hadn't realized that she had been holding it since she had left the back room.

She looked around. In the left corner, behind a row of shelves, was another fire door. She had thought she had seen it before, but hadn't been sure until she had gotten closer. Above it, the "Exit" lights blazed brightly, and there was a large stack of chairs in front of it. She couldn't believe that wasn't a fire hazard. At least now she knew that she had an emergency way out. Just keep track of the exits, she thought. She just needed to mentally mark where they were; she may need them.

She peeked around the last aisle. She hadn't realized that the phone overhead had stopped ringing until it started again. Its loud tones vibrated through the overhead speakers and caused her head to throb. How could the people work here with that loud annoying ring all day? No wonder they were going insane in the front of the store, and who wanted office supplies that badly that they needed to keep calling?

Part of her hoped that maybe it was the authorities calling to get in. Wouldn't it be too soon, though? She tried to think about how long she had been in the back room trying to decide what to do. She hadn't thought she had been back there all that long. It couldn't have been longer than ten minutes, could it? Just how long would it take for the police to come? She had no idea how the police responded in the smaller communities. Yes, she had lived there her whole life, or almost, but this wasn't a typical situation. She imagined that once they had gotten her call, they probably would have gotten there as fast as they could.

Five feet down the aisle, she saw that there was a phone. She doubted that she could call out on it, otherwise the high school and college kids that worked there would probably be on it all day long, but she could answer the call coming in. There was still no one in the aisle. She hadn't seen any signs of life since she had started her aisle-hopping. She should be safe to answer the phone. She didn't like it, she was going to be putting herself in the line of sight from the front of the store, but she still had the back fire door. If something came at her, she could still make it out. But, the one guy had a gun. She couldn't outrun bullets.

Just do it, she thought, working up the courage.

She ran to the phone and grabbed it, the handset nearly slipping out of her grasp. The damned thing was slick. She had to fight to control it, as she brought it up to her ear. Her lungs were burning, and she was still fighting to regain her breath. It hadn't been a long run, but she still had to calm herself down.

"Hello?" she whispered. Silence. She could hear her heart pounding in her chest. There was no one there. They must have hung up. After all of that calling, that constant ringing of the phone, the screeching of it as it had cried out for attention over the loud speakers, the damn phone was now silent. She was alone again, left to try and help the people in the front of the store by herself.

So be it. She let her head rest against the cool metal of the shelves, and felt the small trickle of a tear.

In the distance, she could hear a phone ringing. It had to be from one of the neighboring stores, or maybe it didn't even exist. Maybe she was hearing ringing in her mind, and the bells of insanity were calling her name. It didn't matter. She couldn't give in to hope. She had a job, and it was time to do it. She had to help those people. It seemed obvious that no one was coming to help them. She would have to do it on her own.

Then the ring sounded over the speakers. She turned to look at the ceiling, and then looked back at the phone. There was a flashing light for one of the incoming lines. She pushed it.

"Hello?" she whispered again, barely able to hold back the tears that threatened her. Don't give in to hope yet. She still wasn't saved.

"This is Officer Daniels of the Hammond Police. Who am I speaking to?" The man's voice seemed loud, and she wished she could find a way to lower the volume on the phone's handset.

"Specialist Winona Peters of the National Guard. I was in here shopping when the violence started." She was trying to talk quickly and quietly. She thought she heard something rustling the next aisle over so she turned to look. She couldn't see anything.

"What can you tell me about what is going on? Who's in charge? How many hostages?" the officer asked.

"I don't know if anything has changed since I was up front. I ran to back of the store. I don't think there are any hostages. From what I saw, it looked like some kind of mass murder situation. I don't know what to call it. It was cannibalistic. One person started attacking another, and then someone else started shooting. It might be a robbery, but I haven't found any other survivors yet."

"Okay, how many...wait! What the hell!? Someone's coming out. They look like they're covered in..." In the background, she could hear another man shouting.

"Put your hands on top of your head, and get down on the ground!"

"Hold on," Daniels said into the phone.

"Get down on the ground! Now! Get down, or we'll shoot!"

"Winona, we have a woman that just came out. She's covered in blood from the face down."

Winona was shocked. "She had been one of the customers," she said.

"Well, she doesn't look...right. She's not going down, and still walking towards our police line. I need to ask you, have you seen Sheriff Carter? He went in about ten minutes ago."

"I was in the back. I heard a shot not too long ago, but nothing within the last five minutes."

"Stop!" she heard someone shout

"You said this woman was a customer?" Daniels said, his tone tight with concern.

* * * *

The phone cut off with a momentary silence before it was replaced with the long buzz of the disconnection. She pulled the receiver away and stared at it. Behind her, she heard something metal fall to the ground. It reminded her of what a can of spray paint sounds like when you drop it, but she was in an office supply store. They didn't sell paint. And what was going on outside? Had all the people at the front of the store gone out? Was she safe now? She didn't think so, and it didn't sound like the police were going to be coming in to help her anytime soon.

Another of the metal cans fell. She knew it was close, and there was something about that sound. She knew it wasn't paint, but was something similar. There was something about it that tugged at her, trying to make her remember. It wasn't spray paint, but was in a can like that, and it was white. Something...she had seen. Canned air!

What direction had the sound come from? She hadn't been listening for it so she hadn't been paying too much attention to it. Plus, it seemed to echo. Had it been in the next aisle, or three aisles over? It was hard to tell. So why did canned air make a difference? Why had that bothered her?

She vaguely remembered that at the end of an aisle, she had seen the large display of canned air. She hadn't been paying too much attention to it at the time, but she thought that she remembered it one aisle over. Someone was only an aisle away from her!

The hairs on the back of her neck started to tickle and rise, and the air seemed to hum with electricity. Her stomach flipped, and she could feel that little lump of fear starting to grow inside. A tiny voice in her mind started to squeal at her not to look. That little part of her told her that as long as she never turned around, she would be just fine. That whatever was there, she could just ignore it and this would all be a dream. The little squealing voice was her mother's voice, the one that had told her not to join the military, or date boys. That little voice, that was always afraid for her and had never wanted her to grow up, was also the terrified voice that had screamed at her when she was overseas. She was alive many times over because she listened to that little voice. It was often frightened and often too judgmental, but it had always warned her of danger. And now the voice was telling her she could just stay there and wait. She would wake up, and she would be safe. That it would all be over.
She knew the voice wasn't right this time.

Some kind of chattering sound came from behind her, closer than she would have expected, and she spun to face it. She couldn't stop the gasp that escaped her. She was not trained for it, or shown how to handle what was standing there. She was not ready for it because what she saw should not have been possible. It was inhuman. This couldn't be happening; it had to be a nightmare.

She recognized the man that was standing there. Not only had she seen him not more than twenty minutes earlier, but she had also seen him many times when she had come into the store. He had been one of the men who had helped her when she and her husband had bought their computer. He had helped them get a good deal on it and, when it had a virus, he had helped them get it to a guy that could fix it. He was almost always at the store. He and his large smile, friendly face and beard always made her think of a large teddy bear.

She knew that he had been attacked not twenty minutes ago. His throat had been torn wide open. That friendly smile, those warm blue eyes, she had seen them as the man had fallen back. It was his face, his eyes, his teddy bear frame, but he wasn't the same. Those eyes were now looking at her. It was hard to even imagine them as they had been before.

He stood at the end of the aisle, his large frame taking up most the aisle between her and the fire exit. If not for the barest traces of recognizable features, it would have been impossible to say who he was. There was no kindness there now. There wasn't any sign of humanity, no signs of any kind of emotion. It wasn't him; he was wrong.

Looking at him, looking through the gore that was left of his face, she couldn't stop herself from honing in on his eyes. Maybe she just wanted to avoid looking at the rest of his face because you couldn't even call it a face anymore. His neck had a lot of the muscle exposed and, in some places, she could see down to the bone. The double chin that he used to have was gone. Now, there were large holes where flesh had been torn away. The bottom half of his chin was exposed with pieces of flesh still hanging off, strands of skin barely held in place.

He was covered in blood. The red liquid that had once flowed through his veins had stopped pouring out of him. It looked like most of it was on his shirt. The once powder blue shirt was nearly black from the pure volume of it. It was all down him, soaking the khaki pants and still dripping down onto the tiled linoleum floor. Where he had stopped, she could see little puddles of it.

She looked back to his eyes, and felt a stab of fear at seeing that cold, lifeless gaze looking at her with no signs of the gentleness that used to be there. That glow he had before, the smile while helping them with their computer, was gone now. Those eyes were dead. They were gray and, even though they looked directly into hers, there was no life behind them. She did not feel like he was watching her with them, or that he was even still there.

A gurgling sound escaped from the gap below its jaws. It's as if he was no longer a living man, but had become an "it". The sound that escaped it didn't strike her as a breath; it felt more like a rush of air that escaped the unused lungs. There was no intake of air following it.

It took another staggering step towards her and, somewhere in the back of her mind, a little voice started to pull at her awareness. She needed to stop watching it. She was repulsed by it, but she just couldn't stop staring. She wasn't sure what it was, but she knew it wasn't human anymore.

Somewhere in the front of the store, she started to hear gunfire. Flashes of combat broke through her thoughts, and it was like a firecracker exploding through her head. The speed of the thoughts overwhelmed her as she noticed that it was coming towards her, that it was blocking her path, and that there was gunshots coming from the front of the store.

She had to think. She had to come up with a way out of there. No, that wasn't right. She had no time to think. It was time to act. She would think about it later.

The thing took another staggering step towards her. It was getting really close and was only a few feet away. The creature seemed to also realize this because he leaned forward. She didn't think that it was afraid to fall over if it meant that it would fall onto her. She couldn't allow that to happen, and her body knew what needed to done.

Her basic training came back to her and, in a textbook move, she moved quickly to her left. Then, with a loud angry yell, she brought her right leg up and slammed it down onto its outstretched leg. There was an audible snap, and she felt its knee pop. In an improvised move, she twisted her body, and brought the remaining force down in a punch to its jaw.

The thing was falling back. She wanted to celebrate her triumph, but she had thrown all her weight into the blows she was falling with him.

She continued to react. She wasn't a fighter, but she knew she had to become one or she wasn't going to get out of there. She had to keep moving. She fell into him, there wasn't anything she could do to prevent it, but as he slammed to the ground and then continued onto his side, she came down on top of him. From the hole under his chin, another rasping burst of air escaped. She let out a loud grunt of her own.

She rolled with it, sliding off of the fallen corpse. She hit the cold linoleum, the feel of it sending shivers along her arms. She kept rolling. She knew she wanted to use as much of the momentum as possible. Something deep inside of her had a vague memory of doing that kind of roll down hills when she was a kid, but she pushed it away from her mind. She couldn't allow herself to get distracted now.

She came to a stop when she slammed into one of the metal bases of the shelf. Her head seemed to still roll, and her stomach wanted to heave its contents back onto the floor. She wasn't about to allow it because she couldn't stop now. All she had to do was make it to the door.

She pushed herself up onto her knee and reached out for a shelf as she stood. The door was only thirty feet away so she should be able to make it. There was nothing there stopping her. She was free.

She looked back to see that it had already turned towards her. It wasn't even trying to walk; it was hurrying. That face was still deadpan, and had no pain registration. What it did have was speed, and it wanted her.

She went to step forward, but her leg was trapped behind her. Then she felt it. The vice-like grip of its hand as it grabbed for a better hold on her ankle. Oh, hell no, she wasn't going to go down like this.

In a move that seemed right at the time, she lowered her hands to the floor and put all her weight on them.. Then, thrusting out her other leg, she slammed into his face. She had no way to really aim the thrust because her center of gravity was off, but she felt a solid connection.

She heard the cracking sound of cartilage, and knew that what had been left of its nose was crushed. She came down on her knee, and bolts of pain shot up her leg. Her teeth clinched and ground in agony, and she hoped that the iron taste in her mouth wasn't blood. She didn't have time to think about it. She had to keep going.

She pulled at her leg again. She was using all the strength that she had left. Her head felt like it wanted to explode, and she could feel the warmth of all the blood flooding towards her brain. If she didn't get away soon, this whole experience was going to give her a stroke.

Sparks seemed to cloud her vision, she clinched her teeth, but she still wasn't pulling away from the large man. His hand still held her ankle, and she could feel him pulling her closer.

She chanced a quick look back at him. She must have kicked him in the lower jaw because it now just hanged there with only a small amount of flesh keeping it from falling to the ground. She brought her knee up, this time getting herself ready for a more strategic kick. She didn't know how much it would help. The other kick would have seriously hurt someone if they were still alive, but the blow didn't seem to even slow it down.

That's when she saw them. She didn't know how she hadn't seen them before. They just seemed to be everywhere, black little spiders racing towards her. She swatted at one coming towards her hand. Even as she was doing that, three more were getting closer. Behind them, she could see just over a dozen more coming. Some were going for her upper body, but others were going for anywhere that she touched the floor. A small army of them were nearing her knee, and twice that were heading towards her other hand on the ground. She looked around. They were everywhere.

Pain flashed through her ankle, and she quickly twisted around to look behind her. As she did, she lost balance and rolled onto her butt. It had let go of her ankle as she had lost her balance. Then she saw why it had let go. It had used its upper jaw to dig into the muscle just north of her ankle, and tear away a large chunk of it.

She saw the blood before she realized what had happened. It was gushing out of her and quickly flowing across the tiled floor. She stared at it, her brain not registering what it was. After all, none of this was making sense. Why was there a big hole in her flesh?

She noticed that the spiders had changed direction. They were no longer charging any flesh that was on the ground. They were going towards her leg. No, they were going into her leg!

She quickly thrashed her legs away, kicking out. She was partly aiming towards the corpse, as it was still crawling towards her, but she guessed it was now trying to claw up for better real estate to try and bite into. After all, a leg is nice to start with but just like eating chicken, eventually you want to get to a thigh or breast.

Again, she kicked out, and aimed at his head. She connected, but there wasn't much strength behind it and its head barely rocked back. With a gurgling-like groan, it continued to crawl towards her, and she continued to crawl back.

She was getting closer to the door. It was still several feet away, but she couldn't think about that. She had to keep going. She was almost there, right?

"No matter what," she told herself, "you're almost there." Blood was pooling near her leg, and it was getting hard to lift and to push with it. "Just a little farther away. Come on, just a little bit farther."

She didn't want to look over her shoulder, but it was hard not to. It was getting closer to her. It would reach out, pull against the floor, and inch closer. More spiders were falling from where its jaw used to be. They were landing in her blood, and following it towards her.

Then, it reached out its hand and she felt it grasp at her upper leg. Its grip was like iron. It used it to pull itself closer to her. Either that, or she was being pulled backwards. Something didn't feel right in her head. She felt like a cloud was sneaking in behind her eyes and, as much as she tried, she couldn't seem to find her way through it.

She barely felt it as it used its upper mouth, the teeth that were still there, and bit down. It tore through her jeans and ripped into her flesh. She wanted to scream, and maybe she had. It all seemed like it was drifting away, and she was floating.

Pain? What was that? Instead, she just felt like she wanted to close her eyes and let it take over. It was already too late. Just lay back and give in to it. Just let it...